A PLAN OF WAR

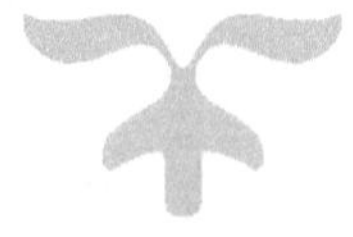

Three Belle's Publishing

By: Donna Emerich

While reviewing who had signed up to join them for the war, Rosie wondered what Henry truly wanted out of all this. After thinking for a minute, she realized that having Deana in office would benefit him. Deana would be told how to vote on certain upcoming issues, and by putting Deana Jay into office, Henry would remain the head of the firm.

There would be a clash between Rosie and Henry—this had already been foreseen. Each faction brought with it both help and problems. The show Deana put on at the Country Club would be a Sore, contentious point with Henry's board of directors. Henry also, knew that the wording about "no mixing" would cause a burn in Deana J.'s saddle, So, to speak.

"Starting off by looking to the stars," Rosie gently touched Denny's shoulder.

“And so, it begins. Plans for war will be necessary to accomplish the goal,” Rosie said Softly. “I know you have concerns, but we know what our word means to those men. Sending them straight to hell still rings in their ears.”

“I understand how you feel about the war,” Denny replied, “but those self-centered pricks thought nothing about ordering our demise for no other reason than we wanted to homeschool our children. We wanted to live life on our own terms. The love of family is the greatest thing to have.”

“They flat-out murdered Fly for pulling a comb from his back pocket. Your job as a junior senator is to go through all the paperwork and find out who signed off on the murder of our family.”

“Let’s slow down. Let’s slow this down a bit,” Rosie said. “From what I understand, governors don't have the juice to make that Sort of decision, which means a senator signed off on it."

"They killed that poor reporter who tried to tell our truth," Deana replied. "Think about his family. There was no reason for his death. A hard pill to swallow. Reporters are seekers of the truth."

As tears fell from Deana's eyes, she had vivid memories of how Sally Jean was treated. The townspeople she knew had been tortured and abused at the hands of Jimmy Joe Ellsworth. No one offered a helping hand, not even the police. So, when her mind finally said enough, she began treating people the way they had treated her. The locals blamed her.

When the sheriff came to deliver her bench warrant, she chose to go out on her own terms and leave a reminder for all to see. What had once been a beautiful home became a hole where her place had stood. Dressed in her wedding gown from Gary, she was ready. The dead-man switch sent them all to their graves on her terms.

"So, Deana," Rosie continued, "we have always been prosecuted in one form or another. These events are what you need to keep in the back of your mind as you look for evidence of who signed off on our deaths."

Hanging her head, Deana knew they were all depending on her—but she had to get elected first.

Rosie gave her a reassuring hug. "We are in this together."

Chris added, "Children were never used as Soldiers in our country."

Thinking for a moment, Rosie cleared her throat. "I do not want to put a rifle in the children's hands, but they still need to be trained in case there ever needed."

The air rushed out of Deanna's mouth like she'd been gut-punched. "Rosie... the idea is repulsive. But even rolling bandages or helping prepare for injuries—arming our children must be a last resort."

Curtis stood in the shadows, listening to the conversation. Even though he had never known Sally Jean, he could feel the pain she had suffered. He didn't remember being picked up or where they lived, but bullies have a way of finding your worst fear and capitalizing on it.

In Sally Jean's case, because she accidentally killed a kitten while trying to feed it milk, her own parents pawned her off on Ma.

Ma showed her that life is important and death is beautiful. Jimmy Joe treated her terribly. He cheated with everyone and anyone, and the misery showed in Sally Jean's face. So, no one thought it odd when he ran off with Some girl who was pregnant by him, never to return.

Thinking about the treatment the family had endured, Curtis understood why this war was necessary. Vengeance was the only punishment that would be accepted.

As Curtis and Deana headed back from the compound, the silence was deafening.

Kaylin proudly announced, "We have new friends! Mama, did you help those people So, their kids will get presents from Santa?"

"Sort of," Deana said. "By helping their parents get the pay they deserve, the parents can pay bills and buy food—and maybe presents too."

Bobbie Sue snuggled against her. “I’m glad you aren’t mean like that Millie lady.”

“Why, thank you, honey. But we need to pray they learn kindness and empathy.”

“I know Sometimes they’re just bad. I do understand, Bobbie Sue.”

“Elsie says to do what you did.”

“Well, thanks for the vote of confidence. Let’s just see if I get elected.”

“Mama, everyone loves you just like we do.”

Something between a laugh and a cry escaped Deanna. “Thanks, girls.” She whispered, “Talking them into it was the easy part. Home base… I don’t want to crush their enthusiasm, but with Henry and the board of directors pushing back, it will be an uphill battle.”

"So, what happens next?" Curtis asked.

"I must put in the notice to run for public office. How are you gonna keep Rosie on the sidelines?"

Curtis sighed. "I believe that if Henry keeps his word, she will too. But if she even thinks he's playing dirty, the gloves will come off, and she'll make him Sorry he was ever born. So, at this point, it's wait and see what happens."

"I need to hit the rack, boss. We start again in the morning," Rosie said.

Curtis seemed a bit nervous—scared, even. From his perspective in the war, he always knew who the bad guys were. It wasn't So, easy to tell when they were wearing three-piece suits and considered the good guys.

"Never judge a book by a pristine cover," Rosie added. "It means it's never been enjoyed. Now get Some sleep. Today was a victory, but I jotted down Some ideas on what we stand for and what could help local communities. I'll leave them on your briefcase. Goodnight."

As Deana readied herself for bed, she had an uneasy feeling—almost like she was being watched. Grabbing a flashlight and a sidearm, she walked the perimeter. Nothing was disturbed.

Behind her, Curtis crept up and whispered, "What's up, boss?"

"I felt like Someone was watching me. I thought Someone was out back, but I found no disturbances. This brings back memories of Jake and his cronies trying to intimidate us."

Curtis nodded. "Well, he's dead, So, we know it's not him."

"That doesn't mean the bodies aren't still pissy with me," Deana muttered.

Heading back toward the house, they saw Rosie standing on the front porch, holding a double-barrel shotgun. Then Curtis noticed a brave on horseback, taking slow steps toward them. JB announced himself.

"Heard voices," JB said. "So, we figured we should check out the area. Our friend isn't good with English, but he knew enough to know they meant harm. He brought me to listen to their plans."

Rosie smiled. "Seems our inventive friends knew you were in trouble and wanted to protect you. And we should be protecting them."

Deana nodded, understanding exactly how she felt.

JB explained what he heard. “You know—just good old boys testing the waters to see if you could defend yourself.”

“Maybe the kids should spend time at the compound,” Deana said.

Looking at JB, Curtis knew how protective Deana was when it came to the children.

“I can see the girls spending time with the other children from each faction. They’ll become each other’s friend-slash-Soldier, standing together as a unit.”

Curtis continued, “I can also, see extra cadet training being needed, along with traveling in pairs or as a group. No more going alone until we figure out who has a problem with me.”

Sunrise came early for Monday morning. At 7:00 AM, Rosie called Henry’s home phone.

"Who the hell," Henry started. "Which Son of a—who is this?"

Clearing her throat, Rosie answered, "That's no way to talk to your friend, Henry."

"Rosie? Yes—Rosie, it's me. How in the hell did you get my home number?"

"It wasn't difficult. Plus, I went through our girls' roll with eggs."

Being out of sight, Henry asked, "What can I help you with?"

"One of our Braves from the reservation heard Some men in town talking. He didn't understand all the slang, but he knew the tone was threatening, So, he grabbed JB to listen. We thought Someone was prowling around. It brought back memories of Jake and his crew's intimidation tactics."

Thinking back, Curtis remembered the rude awakening Jake and his crew once got.

"Henry, our potluck went well," Rosie continued. "Most everyone is on board with Deana being in public office. But imagine our surprise hearing what the men in town were saying. I would ask that she not be penalized if she's late. She didn't sleep—her eyes closed at sunup."

"Okay," Henry replied. "She needs to see me in the office to look over the announcement of her running for office."

"Rosie also, feels the kids should spend time at the compound," Curtis added. "The easiest way to get to Deana is through her children. And since you're going to manage this, you need to be prepared for questions about Deana. You need to understand—our girl will never ask for help."

"Understood, Rosie. Thank you for letting me know. What about last night?"

While cooking breakfast, Rosie told the girls, "Don't disturb Mom. She had a long night. Curtis too."

"Yes," Kaylin said. "They heard noises and checked the perimeter."

"Wow, Aunt Rosie, you know cadet terms."

"Yes," Rosie smiled. "I had family in the military."

"So, you know how to march?"

"Yes, I know my left foot from my right foot."

Giggling, Kaylin said, "The boys don't have rhythm."

"Don't laugh," Rosie replied. "My brothers and I took dance and gym class, So, they can march too. Uncle Rusty doesn't practice marching with us—he prefers the hunting aspects of being prepared. Hunting was Something all my brothers enjoyed as kids."

"Fishing too, Aunt Rosie?"

"Yes, Bobbie Sue, they liked fishing too. We learned how to cook over an open fire for our camping test. I'm sure you girls will be a great help to Rusty and Leroy."

"Can Aunt Lenny camp too? She always got the biggest fish and cooked over an open fire."

Lenny listened to their questions, a smile spreading across her face as she thought, *those girls are mine*.

As the horn honked, the girls ran for the bus.

The noise woke Curtis. Heading for the kitchen, he realized he would be late. Running in, he saw Rosie standing at the door.

“Deana is still sleeping,” Rosie said. “I called Henry and explained last night’s events, and that you two would be late.”

Curtis whispered, “You called Henry at home?”

“Yes. He was not pleased about his early morning call. Once I explained things, he understood. He’ll need her to be okay with the announcement written for her run for public office.”

Deana had heard all the talk, even the girls’ questions. “Rusty has two left feet,” she muttered. “Dance class for gym he did not enjoy, but square dancing he could manage.”

“So, you called Henry at home, Deana?”

“Yes,” Rosie said. “He reacted exactly like that.”

They laughed.

"Oh Lord," Deana groaned. "I know—I need to see him, correct?"

"Yes. Approval of your big announcement. Now, get dressed. Or do I need to do that for you too?"

"No thank you, Aunt Deana."

As Deana dressed, she knew this meant another slow day, maybe with extra time to think.

This morning Curtis shot Deana a look that asked, *"So, what are we? Fired?"*

"Well," Deana said, "if Rosie spoke with him after calling him at home, I imagine backlash will come loudly. But Rosie mentioned an announcement. I would think it's my candidacy."

"So... he's actually going to sponsor you for junior senator?"

"Yes. If Rosie stays off the campaign trail." Taking a final sip from her coffee cup, she added, “Let’s go get our morning ass-chewing from Henry and the board.” The silence was deafening as they drove to town.

“Boss, are you angry that Rosie called Henry at home?”

“Yes and no,” Deana answered. “Yes, because she should leave his domicile alone. That should be a sanctuary from the outside world. And no, because she wanted to show Henry he could be gotten to at home.”

“Christ... do you know why?” Curtis asked.

“In Curtis, it’s a chess match between those two. He could have hung up, but he chose to stay on the line. So, he knows she will be his match—and no one likes to lose.” Pulling into the parking lot, Curtis mumbled, “Here we go again.”

"Stop it, Curtis. You're a war veteran from Vietnam. You eat danger for lunch."

Laughing, Curtis realized he was being silly. Arriving at the second-floor main lobby, the buzz was almost unnerving. Nodding to Julie and Savannah, he asked, "What's going on?"

"Heard you had company last night," Savannah said.

"Yeah," Deana replied. "Some guys in town were talking about me needing to 'learn my place.' One of our Indigenous friends told JB, and they came out to warn us. So... not much sleep."

"That is definitely an understatement," Julie said.

"I feel Sorry for whoever was caught," Deana continued. "Curtis and I were both armed, and our matriarch stood on the front porch with a shotgun in hand. All of this means the boys are upset that I'm not controllable and obviously not taking orders from the male population. We'll do perimeter checks after lights out. I know I ruffled feathers by getting people paid what they were worth. Plus, we took out Jake and his tyrannical mom, So, I'm sure that makes me a threat—not a crusader—to them. It's an old-boy network here. I won't stand for it."

"You're being summoned to the meeting," Savannah said, as Deana and Curtis opened the conference room doors, the room fell silent. Henry nodded to Deana to take a seat. Curtis stood behind her with his back against the wall position he always took when in the hot seat.

"How are you?" Henry asked.

"Well, we're fine, but thank you for asking," Deana replied.

Henry leaned back. "You can imagine my surprise hearing Rosie on the other end of the phone. She went through your Rolodex for my home number."

"Yeah... she really did that. I'm Sorry she disturbed you." "At first I was angry," Henry admitted, "but after she explained what had transpired, I understood it was a courtesy call before they took action."

Nodding, Deana reminded him, "When I first arrived, Jake and his buddies thought intimidation would work. Those boys got quite a surprise. I expected running for public office would be reminiscent of a dogfight."

Smiling, Henry said, "A good rival does spice things up in our little burg. You knew my reputation before hiring me. I make no apologies for who I am. Your success is because you go to the mat for a client. That's why you'll do a great job as a junior senator. Dirt doesn't bother you. So, I'm asking—do you want security at your home?"

Smiling, Deana said, "Is that a rhetorical question? You saw my proficiency with a gun. The family members are better than me. Curtis is a decorated combat vet. I have no worries about my safety."

"What about your children?" Henry asked, still smiling.

"I teach the cadet classes. And Deana's girls are good cadets. Plus, Lenny oversees training. Her PT makes SEAL training look easy."

"Wow," was all Henry could manage. "Rosie just got cleared to start PT," Deana added, "and she'll be back to normal quickly."

One of the board members spoke up. "I have Some questions."

"Well, go ahead and ask."

"I've heard Something about a mountain being blown up."

Thinking a moment before answering, Deana began, “Many years ago, there was an incident. Even though the townspeople paid dearly for it, they never quite got over it. All this family wanted was to live by their own rules and not be bothered. When they applied to homeschool the kids, the town said they weren't smart enough.

They sent CPS and cops up the mountain. Standing toe-to-toe, Fly reached for his comb in his back pocket. They thought it was a gun, and he was killed along with others in the family.”

She continued, “Then the governor sat with the senator and signed off on bombing the mountain. Unfortunately for them, they weren't planning on the family fighting back. The kids were sent to start a new compound. Lenny whipped that ghost town into shape. They pulled a nap-and-snake maneuver and blew their beloved mountain up. Somewhere, hiding in an old coal mine, they were rescued and fixed up. They eventually joined Lenny here."

"There was a reporter doing a story on the family once," Deana added. "He told the truth about the oppressive behavior toward them.

He was killed for telling the truth. The scream of 'Send them straight to hell' still echoes." The board members shook their heads. They now understood why she was a crusader.

"What about the niece—Sally Jean?" another board member asked.

"She was a niece and was married to Jimmy Joe Ellsworth, who was an abusive prick," Deana said. "He beat her constantly. He would bring other men home in front of her. She once mentioned wanting a baby—he beat her stomach to make sure it didn't happen. People thought she wasn't right in the head."

Deana continued, "When she was very young, she had a kitten. She tried to feed it. When it didn't drink from the hole she made, she pushed its little head in too far and it drowned.

Her parents freaked out and gave her to the old lady to raise. Ma taught her many things, including that death was beautiful. After one particularly bad beating, she came out of the hospital different deciding to repay their 'kindness.'"

"Okay," Henry said, "let's not delve into what she did or didn't do. But the end... that was what she considered right."

"There was a bench warrant issued because she didn't show up," Deana said. "When the sheriff arrived to serve her, she opened the door in her wedding gown, hit a dead-man switch, and blew the house off its foundation."

"So, they had been planning for a war," a board member murmured.

"They will never start it," Deana said, "but they'll be more than happy to end it."

"So, what happened to your husband?" Someone asked.

"Dean didn't completely come home," Deana said quietly. "He couldn't hold a job. Drugs and alcohol were an issue. I couldn't leave the girls with him either. Fly overheard me say, 'I wish he'd just go away.' After seeing Dean in action at the bar, Fly spiked his drink with LSD. He figured Dean would end up in jail or Something. What Fly didn't count on was the number of drugs and alcohol Dean had already consumed. He had a psychotic break."

She sighed. "He's made Some improvement, but he has no idea who we are. I got reports from Nurse Charlotte about his progress, but his doctor doesn't feel he should be moved. It could undo everything. So, he'll stay there. His mom is local, So, she visits. My last report said they tried life-skills training for a job. Dean used the tools to assault others in his class."

She looked around the room. "There's much more, but I believe you've heard enough to understand. I hope you have a new appreciation for my crusader status. I lived with these people. I saw their struggle. I became a lawyer to help poor people get a shot at having a life. Criminal defense—because I saw firsthand what happens when clients get assigned a lawyer who thinks 'poor' means 'ignorant.' Speeches like that—heartfelt—is what you'll get from me if elected."

Henry nodded. “This is why you’re well received by the public. Anything we should know about? Criminal arrest record?”

Laughing, Deana said, “No.”

“Now that we’ve gotten to know you a bit,” Henry said, “we can start on your campaign. Here is your public announcement to be aired on the local news this evening.”

Reading through the mock-up, Deana groaned. “Christ, Henry. You make me Sound like a mix between a crusading lawyer and Annie Oakley.”

Henry smirked. “I thought you believed in truth in advertising.”

“I do, Henry.”

“So, we’re using it to prove that what they see is what they get—total transparency. When you’re completely transparent with the public, it gives you a reputation of honesty and awareness. If you have skeletons to hide, the public will sniff them out."

He leaned forward. "If you ever tell her this, I'll deny it—but Rosie is the perfect lady to run your campaign. She's honest, unapologetic, and that holds water with the local folks. We can use the fact your husband is disabled, that you're of rank in the Army National Guard, plus you're an outstanding lawyer for the people. These are great points for your campaign."

"I was thinking about Rosie's potluck too," Henry added.

Deana gave him a skeptical scowl. "And what about her potluck?"

"Most candidates do boring fundraisers—chicken dinners, if you will. But the potluck brought different factions together and won them over with togetherness. Your manifesto needs to be part of your campaign."

"Sir, that was a private Sunday dinner."

"Did they or did they not say they would vote in your favor?"

"...Yes."

"Then use it. Plus, the town meeting over Jade—you're a slam dunk."

Curtis shifted. "You still have townsfolk who view her as a threat."

"Yes," Henry said. "A threat to their financial aspirations. Look, Curtis—our crusader doesn't believe in a free ride for those who already have money."

"What about your parents, Deana?" a board member asked.

"They were what you'd call middle class. Dad worked three jobs Sometimes, but we were an average small-town family. Mom stayed home."

“And your siblings?”

“My brother is a doctor and researcher. My sister works and is a housewife. Just average people in a small town.”

“Good. Curtis—how about you? Anything we should know?”

“No. My family is from New York City. Mom taught school. Dad was in construction. My brothers are both in the military, and my sister is a profesSo,r—women’s studies.”

“Great. No bank robberies?”

“No, sir. I was vetted for the military, and I can pass a background check.”

Laughing, Curtis added, “Maybe you can convince Lenny I don’t live on collard greens and cornbread. I’m not a Southern Black man.”

Henry smiled. "I'm sure she tried hard to understand you."

"Oh, she certainly did," Curtis said. "For Sunday dinner she went to the library, found recipes she thought I'd enjoy—collard greens, ham hock, pinto beans, cornbread. I had trouble getting her to understand—"

Deana cut in, laughing. "Curtis told them they hunt humans like everyone else hunts animals. He was horrified."

"At least that's why they're good," Curtis muttered.

"Oh, priceless," Henry said. "When you're loved by the family, you get special treatment."

"Jesus Christ," Henry added, shaking his head. "I can't decide which side of them is less scary."

Curtis cleared his throat. "It's best to stay on their good side."

"Remember, Jake and his buddies thought Gina would be easy pickings, and the boys' set traps."

"Oh, crap. They forgot about that—about welcoming committees. They give as good as they get, and that was mild compared to what they're capable of."

Henry smiled. "Deana, now that I've heard what we consider skeletons in the closet... should Rosie have all those skeletons out dancing, she'd have no problem with it." He read aloud the law firm's announcement about her running for public office. "Now I'll show you why we're backing you."

With a note of sarcasm, Gina said, "You mean it's not because I'm a great lawyer?"

As if on cue, an intern came in carrying a large stack of papers and set them on the table.

"Seems Someone has been campaigning," Henry said. "But truly, Henry, I haven't announced anything," Deana replied.

"Seems a petition has been circulated. It has over ten thousand signatures from all local counties. You, my crusader, are a very popular member of our firm. Even the Indigenous members have signed on the dotted line. You have the hearts and minds of all the local committees. There are more petitions, but I figured this was a good example to share with you and Curtis. So, buckle up, Crusader—this is going to be a hell of a ride. We'll announce at 3:00 PM, So, bring your smile for the cameras."

Curtis straightened. "Yes, sir. Full dress uniform. Show your status."

"Because I am Black, sir? No military equals no honor? Protection of our community as well as our country?"

Deana smugly asked, "Are you going to dress me too?"

Henry smirked. "Full dress uniform also, they know you're smart, but the uniforms will show strength of character. Your plans are to show you in different styles, providing voters with a secure feeling. Trustworthy, as well as a family matriarch in your own right."

Curtis added, "We used the pictures from your wall to show the Solidarity between you and Deana. The Soldiers will bring your daughters' cadet uniforms. This will show you believe in them—even your daughters are military."

"Here's you at the motor pool helping the guys," Henry continued.

"So, basically, I'm Wonder Woman?" Deana laughed.

Henry chuckled. "We need to capitalize on all your strengths. You're a country girl—most women will value that."

"Okay, Henry. I believe you've planned this out, but it Sounds like a Rosie campaign."

"After speaking with her at 6:00 AM, I decided to take a page from her book. I believe your manifesto is 'God, Guns, and Family.' I took the liberty of asking for a copy."

"Why?" Deana asked.

"Let's just say I needed clarification on intention. Your intention is to give everyone a voice. I hate admitting this, but your idea was brilliant, and people seemed genuinely happy when they left your office. Your intuition is spot on. So,

I'll give you three twelve-hour days here. Two days you can work on your appearances. No Q&A or TV appearances unless I vet them first. Reporters are well known for changing questions."

"I've also, decided we could use Some of Rosie's talents at rallying people to come together and fight."

He waved her off. "Go answer your phone messages. I need to get all the stations to send reporters for your announcement. Have everyone here by 2:30 PM."

As Deana and Curtis headed to the third floor, both had questions.

"So, what did Rosie and Henry bond over?"

"No idea, but I'm sure Rosie encouraged him to trust her. They both want the same thing—me in office."

Curtis shook his head. “Same goal, different reasons. I think Henry believes he can control it all. As if he can befriend Rosie.

That’s like being friends with a mountain lion with a wine purse. If I had to fight one, Lenny would be tough. She’d enjoy it too much.”

Henry was standing behind Curtis when he interjected, “Lenny doesn’t look scary to me.”

Deana turned to him, eyes alive. “Never underestimate a female from the family. They will patiently wait until your guard is down, then devastate and destroy you before you realize what happened. I’d pit Rosie against any man. She learned at the knee of my Ma—no better strategist. The boys tend to be more physical and hands-on.”

“So, Crusader,” Henry asked, “who did you learn from?”

"All of the above, Henry. I never questioned the matriarch's wisdom. Curiously, I never had the pleasure of meeting Ma. But if that's who trained Rosie, I concede to her knowledge."

"You might want to remind those boys they walked out of a maximum-security prison," Deana added. "They know how to play the game."

Henry nodded. "I understand. Their lack of defense should've raised red flags. I could've presented a better defense as a teenager. There should be a law against appointing lawyers without criminal experience for a trial."

"Let me guess," Deana said, "that was sewn up before the trial ever started. That's why you were So, hell-bent on Jake's trial?"

"If I hadn't been So, diligent in my research, he'd have walked. His mama had money, intimidation, bribery, whatever officials she needed. If people would take that, Jake's family would keep the criminal justice system uprooted."

"I need to do Some work before 3:00 PM, if you don't mind."

After answering several phone calls, Deana looked at the clock and sighed. "I need to get home for my dress uniform."

Julie knocked. "There are two ladies out here, and they have your dress uniform and a picnic basket."

"It's fine, Julie. Let them in."

Lenny peeked in. "Hey! Curtis has an office now."

Smiling, Deana said, "He's moved up in the world." Looking around, Lenny decided Curtis's office was lacking. While Rosie laid out food, Curtis offered her a hand.

Laughing, Rosie admitted, "It's harder to get off the floor than it used to be."

"What brings you ladies here?" Curtis asked.

"We brought the dress uniforms and lunch because you'll be busy this afternoon. We even brought enough for Henry." Rosie looked to Julie. "Would you be a dear and tell Henry his plate is made?"

"Yes, ma'am," Julie giggled.

"Oh, Curtis," Rosie added, "I added your patches, and I spoke with your superior officer. I got a copy of the awards and where they're placed on the uniform."

"Where did Lenny run off to?" Rosie shook her head. "Not sure."

Curtis then heard a loud ruckus coming from his office. He and Deana sprinted toward it.

Lenny was decorating.

"What are you doing?"

"Oh! I thought your walls were drab, So, I felt these would help." She held up pictures of the compound, Curtis climbing the Victory Tower, teaching cadets, and a heart.

A picture of Curtis, a picture with the family, and a picture of Deana crossing the finish line while Curtis coached her family cheering her on. Henry had a huge, smug grin as he looked at Curtis.

"I believe you are truly family."

Putting her arm through Henry's, Rosie escorted him back to the office for lunch.

"What's this, ladies?"

"Pulled pork sandwiches, macaroni salad, coleslaw, and fresh biscuits with berry pie for dessert," Rosie said. "I brought the kids their dress uniforms, with all the awards displayed properly."

In between bites, Henry said, "I'd like the kids to be in their cadet uniforms."

Rosie nodded. "I've attached their ribbons as well."

"Rosie, did you pass out the petitions?" Henry asked. Knowing the answer, he waited.

Rosie finally explained, "I felt we needed to show you how popular she is with the people—So, I could prove to you that the firm is backing the right candidate."

"Well, as usual, Rosie, your point is well received. If you'll excuse me, I need to finish the arrangements for our girl's announcement."

Looking confused, Deana asked, "Since when are you and Henry buddies?"

"Keep your friends close and your enemies—closer," Rosie said. "No, sir, we will all come to hear you announce your candidacy."

Turning quickly, Henry said, "Thanks, Rosie. Lunch was delicious, as usual."

Curtis's mouth fell open. "Since when does Henry compliment anyone? How did you get him to—?"

"Well, he realizes I'm training him," Rosie smiled. "Before you know it, he'll be taking my orders."

Curtis shook his head and helped pack up the picnic. Carrying the basket to the car, Rosie grabbed her purse.

"It'll be fine. I've positioned myself to help if Henry suddenly changes his mind. I have feelers out. Everyone wants our girl in government."

Curtis looked at Rosie, steadfast. "I don't trust Henry. He wanted to hear all our skeletons—So, no surprises. Isn't that why we send a spotter ahead? So, you don't walk into an ambush?"

"Same principle, Curtis. I don't allow Deana to be Henry's sacrificial lamb. Tell her the girls will be here at 2:30. Henry trusts you. I promise we'll be here. Go back to work."

As the day started to roll, Curtis felt like a prized pig being groomed for slaughter. Now he understood how Claude felt. Even the security guys were treating him differently. It was unnerving.

But here he was in his dress uniform. He thought he'd only wear it for funerals—and his own wedding, with Dean as his best man. Who knew he would fall for his best friend's wife? Dean would never be the same, but Curtis knew he wouldn't either.

All the reasons he loved Deana were the same reasons she earned the title "Crusader." The Crusader—she had an open field of fire against those who wronged the poor. Minimum wage was a joke out here. No one enforced it. God's voice echoed in Curtis's head.

A noise caused him to turn. Rosie was offering to help with those pesky collar buttons.

Smiling, Rosie cooed, "You are a handsome man, Curtis."

"Thank you, Rosie."

"Hi, Curtis!" squealed Kaylin and Bobbie Sue.

"You ladies look great in those uniforms. Well, kids—what do you think? Is that really you?"

"Yes, girls, this is my dress uniform."

"Wow, Mama, look at all those ribbons!"

"It took me a long time to earn these."

"Wow, look at all of Curtis's ribbons!" Kaylin reached up to touch them.

Deana explained, "Curtis was active duty. Some of those are campaign ribbons."

"So, when you complete an assignment, they send you off to help Someone else?" Kaylin asked.

"Yes. When you get a new set of orders, you report to your new post."

"So, if Mom was active duty, she'd have those ribbons too?"

"Yes. Your dad has the same things and ribbons I do."

They smiled.

Curtis continued, "I was going to do this at cadets tonight, but since we'll be on a stage, I thought I'd give you your cadet ribbons—and your expert shot medal, just like your mama."

"Can Mama put them on?"

"I don't see why not."

The shiny medals and ribbons were shown proudly to their extended family.

"Uncle Rusty," Bobbie Sue asked, "is it okay for girls to be good shots?"

Rusty smiled. "Yes. It's half the reason I like your Aunt Lenny—she's a great shot. They're just fine."

Leroy found the conversation amusing.

Rosie roared, "Mirror check!" Everyone lined up. "Single file. Now go out there and show them who the best candidate is!"

Henry stood at the podium, waiting for the crowd to quiet down. He read his remarks about the law firm backing Deana. Then Deana stepped up to the podium.

She introduced Curtis and her daughters, speaking about how important it is for girls to receive the same education as boys. With a proud smile, she bragged about her daughters' success in the cadet program.

Deana began listing the office she was running for, her qualifications, her humble beginnings, and how she grew up.

"Hard work is the only way to achieve your goals. I will not ask anything of you that I would not do myself. And in case you're wondering, I have scrubbed clothes on a washboard, made homemade Christmases, and cooked loads of cheap dinners. I do my own oil changes and repairs on my car. I am no better than you. I want you to succeed—jobs, living wages, fair pay for hard work, and an equal playing field. I am here to represent all of you, not just a select few. Thank you."

A loud, thunderous round of applause ended her speech.

Walking off the stage, Rosie said, "Now you are officially going to be the town savior."

"It's just junior senator, but it gets you in the door."

"I'll take the girls to get ready for cadet class. Thank you for giving them their awards—it made them feel important."

Running in to change for cadets, Curtis was caught in thought, looking at the pictures Lenny had put on his wall. Sadness engulfed him. He knew death would be intimate, knowing what would truly come to pass. Looking at the pictures of his turns—full of pride as he had become a hero—he wondered what his parents would think of Rosie and her family. They had struggled in high school. He had to work three times harder than the next guy to get a break.

"Aunt Rosie says shake a leg!" Kaylyn announced. "She needs to put those dress uniforms away."

Laughing, Curtis shook a leg. Rosie cuffed him upside the back of his head.

"Don't mock me, young man."

"Yes, Mama."

"Excuse me, Curtis."

"Yes, ma'am."

"That's better."

"Just when I think we're on an even field," Curtis muttered, "Rosie reminds me who's running the show."

Handing Lenny the uniforms, Deana tried to answer the mound of phone messages. The militia families were pleased but cautious. They had flown under the radar for years.

This campaign would bring their cause to the front lines. A leader from the reservation called to pledge support. Many new clients worried she wouldn't have time for them.

Deana explained, "You are the reason I'm running. I need to be involved in the lawmaking process—how it affects your lifestyle. The government runs on numbers and money. I need to pursue fair labor practices."

A large sigh came from the other end. "We were worried you'd forget about us, ma'am."

"I would never forget you. I am the Crusader for the poor."

"Ma'am, are those cadet classes lots of money? I'd like my boys to get training."

"No, it's free."

"But what about your daughters? Is it okay for them to go too?"

"Yes. It's good for girls to get training too."

"Guns and everything?"

"Yes."

"Thanks, Miss Deanna."

Curtis added quietly, "As weird as this Sounds... maybe these ladies should be exposed to Lenny and Rosie."

"Geez, why don't you just throw them in with a panther, Deana?" Curtis muttered.

"These ladies have much to offer, but they've been cowed down for So, long," Deana replied. "Maybe they need a reminder of the resolve they already have. Kids have cadets to let off steam—So, maybe the ladies should have their own club or get-together. Time with other women. Men tend to keep their secret fishing holes or hunting spots quiet. Women are naturally more giving, So, they're more willing to talk about what they've experienced and how they overcame problems." Curtis furrowed his brow. "So, crafts to shooting guns?"

"Yes. They need to be useful in an emergency. Triage, if it comes to that. The militia wives already dry meat and canned foods—that's a useful skill. Shooting a gun is necessary too. Example: there's a fight, and you must save your man. If you don't understand the mechanics of the gun, they're dead meat. Bow and arrow practice also, Lenny makes damn good Soldiers, So, I'll put her in charge."

"Okay," Curtis said, "but I find this a bit exasperating."

"You're just used to being in charge. Trust me, you'll be surprised at what Lenny will have them doing. Rosie will agree with me, I assure you. Let's head home. You have new kids to teach."

"Can I take Rusty with me? The brand-new ones—I can start them with safety, and Rusty can take the others who are further ahead."

"Oh, that's a good idea. The advanced kids won't fall behind."

Rusty arrived in full camo gear.

"What's this all about?" Curtis asked.

"Well, they won't be wearing tutus," Rusty said, "So, I figured we'd start using camo in different scenarios to see how they handle it."

"Not bad, Rust. Make sure you remind them of their oaths. This is a team effort, not a single-Soldier show like the militia kids. Maybe a prize for the best marksmanship score. A little healthy competition is good for sportsmanship. These are good skills for all of us to learn."

"What about those ladies?" Curtis asked.

"Rosie and Lenny will be there in force," Deana said. "They'll teach all the important skills. Most of these women have spent their lives having babies and being housewives. A bit of physical training—they'll be Soft, but we need them strong. They'll be the backbone of this operation."

Rosie spoke to her husband in a hushed tone. "We need to train all the women in case fighting comes close to home. So, we start training everyone. Triage will be very important. Lenny, I need you to talk with your buddy at the armory for supplies—bandages, morphine, sutures, etc. Anything you can't get that way; we'll speak with Gilbert about."

"I'm thinking training three times per week," Deana added. "They have family obligations. Once they're used to it, we can step up the pace."

"What about Henry?" Lenny asked.

Rosie smiled. "We'll be more than happy to let Henry think he's in charge. We'll be working behind the scenes."

Laughing out loud, Lenny clutched her stomach. "That poor man has no idea what he's opened the door to.

Once D is a junior senator, she can snoop around and we can find out who that Son of a birch was who signed off on blowing them straight to hell. Then we can return the favor. But it's still a long road—don't get full of yourselves yet. This won't be an easy road."

"You know that Board of Directors will be a thorn in our side," Deana said.

"True. But if I play the game, they won't have a clue."

After a few drinks, Deana began to unwind. Kaylin and Bobbie Sue came running into the kitchen, squealing.

“Mama, guess what!”

“What?”

“We won the target contest! We beat the boys!”

“Well, I am very proud of you.”

“Uncle Rusty says we’re ready for a real rifle—and a bow and arrow too!”

“Oh, I see. Does that mean a trip to the pro shop?”

“We don’t need practice trips, Mama. We hit the bullseye every time!”

Curtis came in dragging. “What happened to you?”

“Those new kids cried when they got a reprimand. They’ll take time to catch up with the other compound kids. Guess we’ll need more supplies. They were afraid to go looking for the arrows. Most can handle PT well enough."

"So, supplies?" Deana asked.

"Practice tips and a couple of BB guns for basic safety procedures. And we need a few tents So, they can practice setting up and taking down camp. Running with packs on and such."

"Okay. Make the list and I'll leave you cash for the expenditure. How did Rusty do?"

"Not bad. He knows the older kids. Next time we'll send Leroy, So, the kids get used to the other leaders. When they graduate to real rifles, I'll let Rosie teach them—she's the best with a rifle or shotgun."

"So, when is your first appearance as a candidate?"

"Henry is setting up dinners and appearances. I'll get a list."

“Kids—bedtime. And Mom is very proud of you.”

“If Dad was okay, would he be proud of us?” Bobbie Sue asked.

“Yes, girls. He would be very proud.”

“Curtis, how long are we cadets?” Kaylin asked.

“Well, we have many things to cover to be a good Soldier.”

“What’s basic training?”

“When you sign up for the military, you take an ASVAB test to see what areas you excel in. Then they give you a list of jobs your scores qualify you for. Then you’re sent to basic training—six to eight weeks of learning to be a Soldier. After graduation, you’re sent to AIT for your job training.”

“So, even in the military you have a job?”

"Yes. We aren't always at war. Everyone has a regular job. Now hit the rack."

"Curtis?"

"Yes, sir."

Laughing, Rosie said, "I couldn't have explained it better myself."

"Would you approve?" Curtis sniped.

"Watch that. I am still the matriarch of this family, and I demand respect."

"A little rough on Curtis, weren't you, Rosie?" Deana asked.

"No. Just reminding him who's really in charge. Get your asses to bed, Crusader. You'll have a long day tomorrow."

"How much fundraising is this role going to take?" Deana asked.

"To be honest, Rosie, I have no idea. If I had to guess—the more money donated, the more ass you have to kiss.

They'll want you to vote on their bill or convince another senator to vote for theirs. Basically, more ass-kissing, less actual work."

"Okay, now I'm nervous. Thanks a lot, Rosie."

Smack.

"What the hell was that for?"

"Respecting my position as matriarch. So,—do you have a plan of action for these ladies?"

"I'll start with coffee and find out how they feel about their roles as wives and moms. We'll do the crafting thing. Triage will be introduced as Something good to learn in case the kids or hubby get hurt.

Same thought process for firearms. They just need other women to talk to. And I think John's wives could use the company."

"Agreed. Goodnight, Rosie."

As the sun rose above the hillside, the smell of coffee wafted through the air. Deana covered her head with a pillow—no real sleep again. She knew Henry would have a list for her. Lots of rubber-chicken dinners to raise funds for her race. She needed a landslide. The old boys already knew who would win before the campaign even started.

"So, who do you think will be viable?" Curtis asked.

Shaking her head, Deana sighed. "I'm overwhelmed with these plans."

Rosie announced, "You'll do just fine. Henry can't force you to go along with him."

"That's not accurate, Rosie. He and the firm can pull their backing at any time."

"Okay—So, choose," Rosie said sharply.

Scowling at her, Deana muttered.

Rosie reminded her, “There are people counting on you to stand up for them. So, what’s truly bothering you?”

“Henry gave way too easy for my liking. I don’t trust him. And the fact that he wants to keep you out of sight doesn’t sit well with me.”

Scratching her chin, Rosie thought. “You think he intends to pull the rug out from under you?”

“It wouldn’t be the first time he set me up to fall on my face.”

Curtis nodded. “I’ve never trusted Henry.”

“Mama!” the girls called. “When do we get to go to the hunting store and get our BB guns? And the bow and arrows too!”

“Well, since you did So, well as cadets, we should celebrate your skills.”

"Can Uncle Rusty take us?"

"Sure—but I figured Curtis and I would take you. But you'll be busy with work and campaigning."

"That's very considerate of you not to bother me, Mama."

"Yes, girls."

"Why do the militia ladies and Indigenous people dry meat or make jerky?" Kaylin asked.

Thinking a moment, Gina explained, "Refrigeration wasn't common back in the day, So, they learned to dry and preserve meat So, it wouldn't rot."

"So, that's why they can food?"

"Yes. Canning preserves food with heat. You fill the jars, add water and spices, seal them, then put them in a canning pot. After the right amount of time, you take them out and listen for the pops—that means they're sealed."

"Wow, that's a lot of work."

"But you'll be glad when it's -30° and there's no food."

"So, only poor people can?"

"No. Middle and upper-class people can too. At least you won't starve."

"So, you know how to can?"

"Yes. My mom always had a large garden. We canned or froze all the vegetables. Pickles were fun—if they didn't seal, you got to eat them."

"Did your dad go hunting?"

"Yes. Deer season was a big deal."

"Girls—the bus will be here. Head outside."

"Sounds like the girls are eager to learn about homesteading," Curtis said.

"See? Country living is good for the girls," Lenny crowed, grabbing a cup of coffee. "So, what's going on, Rose?"

"I think every girl has Some reservations."

"Let me guess—Henry," Lenny said.

"Crowd," Rosie muttered.

"Rosie, how about another potluck—but at the Country Club? That way no one will be uncomfortable."

"Yeah, those rubber-chicken dinners are not my style."

Rusty blurted out, "Henry only has control when he has his money, right? What if we fund it ourselves? Then when she wins—it's not Henry's issue."

"They can't hold those campaign donations over her head."

"Well, holy shit, Rusty, there's really a brain in there."

"Stop. I just don't want to have to answer to those blowhards."

"Family meeting, yo," Lenny called out. "Gathering all the pertinent factions together for a vote."

"So, what's up?"

"Rusty has pointed out that the law firm is backing her for political office, and they hold all the donations. They could end up controlling how she's viewed by everyone. So, Rusty suggested that we use our own funds to keep things balanced and even."

Lenny then popped up with the idea of another potluck at the Country Club for anyone who would like to donate. "Rubber-chicken dinners are not how she needs to be perceived.

Deana is all about her constituents getting treated fairly. That's what she should be known for. We start making flyers and call the Country Club to reserve it."

Clem spoke for the militia, agreeing with the funding aspect.

"So, Curtis is still teaching the hunter-safety course?"

"Yes, he is. Why?"

"Thinking... well, now there's more kids. Maybe he could use Some help."

"That would be very helpful," Rosie smiled. "She will have to score highly for Electoral College."

"So, there has to be an election unless no one runs against her," Clem explained.

"She'll have to run against an established political rival once it's cut down to two. And when there's two left, the gloves come off. That's why Henry asked about skeletons in the closet."

Nodding, Leroy spoke. “I would bet they bring up Dean. Henry spoke with Dean’s doctor in case we could bring him home. Seems when they tried to teach him job skills, he used his tools as weapons. He must be controlled with antipsychotics, plus he has no idea who Deana or the girls are. She’s done everything in the book for his care.”

“He did ask about us. A background check,” Rusty laughed. “They think we’re dead.”

“Hey,” Roy growled. “Not like they didn’t try. That asshole senator gave the OK to the governor. Send them straight to hell.

All that BS came from us wanting to homeschool our kids. So, they used a military maneuver called a ‘Nathan Snake.’ It blew up the mountain, but they got a surprise. We were prepared,” Clem said.

"So, this is the reason you moved here?"

"Yes. We also, explained about our niece, Sally Jean," Rosie added, nodding in agreement.

Clem understood why this was such an important fight for the family. He thought back to the reporter who tried to tell the truth about the family's flight—and it got him killed. Putting their hands together as a move of Solidarity, he said, "Whatever you need us to do, Rosie."

Meanwhile, Deana was quietly working in her office when a light knock Sounded at her door. Julie stuck her head around the corner.

"Henry wants a meeting. Now."

"Alright. Tell him I'll be right there. I'm on the phone with Public Health to get those ladies Some birth control and Some health care."

Curtis whispered, "You're getting called into a meeting."

Nodding, Deana finished her phone call to her client. Heading to the conference room, Deana let out a breath, then opened the doors. Henry was seated with what she assumed was a PR professional.

As Deana seated herself, Henry introduced her as a prospective junior senator. The woman looked Curtis up and down.

"So, who is this—staff?"

Before Deana could speak, Henry informed her of Curtis's medals and service to his country.

"Oh, I mean nothing by it. I was concerned he was your husband."

Watching the color drain from Deana's face, Curtis spoke. "Ma'am, I want you to know that Deana's husband is in a facility. He had a psychotic episode and never came back fully from combat. And I would be proud to be Deana's husband. But Dean was my best friend, So, now I watch over Deana and her daughters. If the shoe was on the other foot, Dean would do the same for me. Are there any questions for me, ma'am?"

"No, Curtis, I understand your position. I am reviewing security roles."

"Sniper," Curtis corrected. "From what I understand, she doesn't need security since I have a copy of her scorecard from her concealed-carry permit." Curtis growled, "So, I have no value. I'm just arm candy." Laughing loudly, Henry said, "I'd be careful. She is tough verbally. Just ask anyone who's her opposition in council."

Looking at Deana, Lola asked, "You aren't going to make my job easy, are you?" "Easy isn't a challenge, is it?" "OK, let's try another subject. We have put you on the ballot. Once competitors drop off, it will be a race between you and the other leading opponent. As of today, there are three of you in the race. Your biggest problem will be your competition. You aren't from here—you're not local—So, we need to make you look more like a valued part of this town."

Curtis asked, "How about the fact that she prosecuted Jake, won in all three courts, and made sure those children will have counseling and a good home away from Jake's family? Or taking the case of the accidental murder over his pig—he got a new piglet and an apology."

"Deana fits in here well. She encouraged the townspeople at the town meeting to take a stand against Jake and his family. Last Sunday she hosted a party at the Country Club showcasing handmade wares. Local merchants were cheating these people—buying items for pennies on the dollar, then marking them up three times and selling them for another profit."

Curtis then bragged with pride about getting poor families health care and birth control. "Can those other pompous asses do better? Let them try."

Lola decided she wouldn't win this argument. "Let's try this. I've taken the liberty of going through pictures of you. Which would you like to use?"

Henry smiled. "How about we use three of them?"

Lifting an eyebrow, Curtis was concerned about his motive.

Lola looked through the photos. "Law school. Henry, use the one in her military uniform, the graduation picture, and the family one with the kids—

showing different facets of Deana's personality and charm."

"OK, Henry, I'll agree to those pictures."

Lola wasn't quite done sharpening her claws. "Is there a picture of Dean?"

"Yes." Curtis ran to his office, grabbing his pictures of them in-country. Looking through them, Lola chose the picture of them watching her law-school graduation and the one of the kids climbing all over the Soldiers.

"All I'm saying is the public must be able to relate to you. Showing them the accomplishments they understand will turn into votes. Now, I understand you have a hillbilly family, your friends with—are they going to be a problem? I'll let Henry explain about his first lunch meeting."

As Henry described the altercation in full color—ending with him dropping

$100 bills and muttering money burns, Lola raised an eyebrow. “Sounds like a colorful bunch.”

Curtis then gave a recap of his first meeting, including the part where “they hunt humans like most hunters hunt animals.” Horrified, Lola looked like Someone had sucked the air out of her lungs.

Then Curtis told her about being called “their good Nagy.” “Christ, Henry,” Lola groaned, “how am I supposed to deal with those rednecks?” Henry cackled. “You wanted the job, sweetheart.”

“It would be easier to sell the mob to this town’s people,” Deana muttered. “But this might be exactly what the town needs. I’m not from here, as you So, gently pointed out, but I’ve learned what matters to these people. They deserve an even playing field. They put their heart and So,ul into handmade items that weren't paid for properly. Many of these families have ancestry dating back to the Civil War."

Henry nodded. "Your great-grandfather became the first sitting judge. He also, started this law firm."

"What I discovered in my visits to the tractor paths, So, to speak," Deana continued, "is that work here is year-round, not seasonal. Roland and March have seven children. Roland makes beautiful hand-carved furniture but had no way of letting people know. Curtis brought Roland over to the furniture company, showed pictures of his work, and he was hired on the spot—plus they bought everything he had stored in his barn. These people need a chance, that's all."

"Now I see how you got the title of 'crusader,'" Lola said, smiling. "This kind of passion is Something I can work with. If you were planning on a Barbie doll, then I'm the wrong girl for you."

"I can see that," Lola added. "Let me work on Some plans and I'll get back to you in a few days."

Deana was exhausted just from talking to PR. "This will be difficult. I'm not going to be a professional guinea pig for the cameras."

Curtis laughed. "At least you're not the token Black man or the war veteran."

Henry announced his presence by saying, "She's abrasive, but she gets the job done. We'll see how she fares with Rosie."

"Smart, Henry," Deana muttered.

Shaking his head, Henry smiled. "I'll send Lola a bottle of Scotch. She's gonna need it."

Deana knew the good-old-boys wouldn't be pleased. Families like Jake's saw her as the new order. This would be a constant issue.

She'd heard So, me of the men didn't want women in charge—nothing unusual for the Western states. "Women don't serve in the military; they stay home and throw luncheons."

Henry soothed Deana's feathers. "They just aren't used to women having So, many male-dominating traits."

"So, what now? You're going to complain I'm not ladylike enough for you, Henry?"

"Not exactly. They've started calling you the Annie Oakley of Montana."

"Hey, they used to call me that," Deana smiled.

"So, how are your new clients?" Henry asked.

"Fine. I arranged for the public-health nurse to go see the kids and the moms."

"Is that because they don't drive?"

"Yes. The men have the vehicles for work or hunting, So, the women don't have access to the family car or truck."

"What about their crafts?"

"I have shopkeepers willing to take items on consignment. Roland is doing well at the custom furniture store."

"Let's head out to lunch and I'll go over my ideas for your campaign strategy."

"OK, you're the boss," Deana cracked.

The lunch crowd had just filled the club's dining area. Taking his usual table, the waitress brought Henry a martini and Deana a sweet tea. Opening his briefcase, Henry laid out a full proposal of dates for speeches. Most looked doable except the weekend guard shifts.

"I'll talk to your superior if necessary. I'm sure he'll understand all of us have outside jobs. But you'll need Curtis for these dates too."

"I can handle myself just fine." "Do I need to hire bodyguards? I'm sure I could get Leroy or Rusty to put on a monkey suit for an evening." "Ladies Auxiliary will be your first speech. After a few weeks of campaigning, we'll do a live debate on camera. Here's a list of topics. Familiarize yourself with them. Here are notes for you," Henry growled.

"Do not go off script. Stay focused on the topics I've outlined. No mention of the family or their plight. No talk of poor people or lack of jobs."

"Sounds a bit one-sided to me, Henry. I won't avoid touchy subjects to make things more comfortable for those of means. You call me the crusader but won't let me do my job."

Food arrived. Henry dove into his club sandwich with a vengeance. Between bites, he tried to plead his case. Deana just listened. None of his ideas suited her personality.

She began formulating her own plans that didn't erase the poor. She nodded half-heartedly for Henry's benefit.

Walking back to the office, Henry asked, "You got quiet. Why?"

"Just thinking about what you said, Henry." She smiled sweetly. "Why, Henry, are you insinuating I'd go against your wishes with a full-on breast-sucking band in the middle of town?"

Laughing, Deana added, "Really? I go to the mat for my clients in every case. What would you expect me to do? I may not always agree with your politics, but I always do my job to the best of my ability. That's why you hired me."

"That is correct, my little crusader. But I didn't know you'd be such a pain in the ass."

"Well, I guess you'd agree you're also, a large pain in the ass," she shot back.

Henry growled. "I am still your boss, Crusader."

"And I am your equal, not your pretty toy. I graduated top of my class. Jesus, Henry—a pissing contest? Really thought you were better than that."

"Well, Sometimes I have to stoop to your level, Miss Crusader."

"Well, now that I know where I stand, maybe Rosie should be my campaign manager."

As Deana walked into the office, she ran up all three flights of stairs. Climbing out of the first stairwell, steam practically coming off her, she was furious.

“Julie, I’ll be out in the field for the rest of the week. I’ll call in for messages.”

Standing behind her, Curtis had heard everything. He knew “out in the field” was an excuse to avoid Henry.

Rosie and Lenny would not take this lying down. The punishment would be brutal. Last time Henry went home after a pow-wow with Rosie, he drank a whole bottle of Scotch. Grabbing folders, Deana headed for the stairwell.

“No elevator, boss?” Curtis asked.

“No. Because if I see Henry, I’ll get arrested. That won’t look good for my campaign, now, would it?”

After visits with the public-health nurse, her clients were in better spirits—but Deana was still fuming about her lunch with Henry.

The drive home was deafening. Naughty words filled the air. Curtis hadn't seen Deana this angry in a long time. The fact that Henry was still standing and breathing was a miracle.

As they pulled into the driveway, Deana noticed tire-tread marks that didn't belong to anyone she knew. Closer to the front door, she saw more strange prints.

"The front door is open," she whispered.

Curtis pulled out his gun and quietly opened the door. He cleared each room. His concern grew—no kids either. They should've been home hours ago.

Deana checked the perimeter, noticing more tracks. No nature sounds. No birds. The silence felt apocalyptic.

"No people around," she murmured. "Let's go out to the compound, Curtis. I feel it in my bones. Something isn't right."

Driving to the compound, Curtis glanced at her. "What's up? This is weird. Your place is never quiet."

"I realize that, Curtis. But I know Rosie and Lenny would protect the girls with their lives. They're all about family."

"I understand that Coach," Curtis said, "but the quiet is creepy."

"I agree."

Pulling up to the compound, the silence was just as unnerving. Opening the front door to the dining hall, they found coffee and bread in the oven.

“Well, they must be around here Somewhere,” Deana said.

“Wait,” Curtis whispered. “Do you hear that?”

The girls were walking in from a field, carrying ferns for cooking.

“They’re called fiddleheads,” Anna explained. “We were worried—the front door was open and there were tracks we didn’t recognize.”

“Sorry about that,” Rosie said. “We were with our Indigenous friends. Those ladies can cook anything.”

Julie had called the house—another fight with Henry. The color of Rosie’s face gave away her opinion. “Plus, that PR chick, Lola, wants to turn you into a politically correct Barbie.”

“I guess we need another meeting with Henry,” Deana sighed.

"I knew letting him be in charge was a bad idea," Rosie muttered. "Let me see the list of dates."

After looking them over, she realized Henry had scheduled the events So, Curtis would be with his guard unit—meaning no security.

"What the hell is Henry up to?" Rosie roared. "He's making our girl a target. Anything goes wrong, she takes the blame. No junior-senator venture. So, who does he plan on putting in your place?"

"When's your next meeting with the PR girl, Lola?"

"She said a few days."

"Well, I need to explain our position about this campaign," Rosie said. "I'm done keeping the peace. And we have a snooper—he stays just outside of sight and watches the house."

"Why would he do that?" Deana asked.

"Because Someone put him up to it. Some of the men in town aren't crazy about your ascension to political office. We'll know more Soon. The militia boys offered to take turns watching the house."

"That was nice of them."

"So, you're out in the field all week?"

"Yes. That's what I want Julie to tell Henry."

"Won't that piss him off?" Leroy cracked.

"Of course it will. That's the point."

"Sounds like you're looking for a fight," Leroy teased.

"More like a showdown. He told me to 'stoop to his level.' He's going to be sorry he said that" Rosie growled. "Can we do things my way now?"

"Yes, Rose. You have the reins."

"Good. I'll make calls in the morning."

As thoughts danced in Rosie's mind, Henry officially became the enemy. But careful, polished planning was needed. Rosie was tough, but she never allowed anyone to mistreat family—and Deana Jay would always be family.

Curtis listened as the events of the day unfolded. He knew he couldn't get out of guard weekends either, So, he'd have to trust Leroy or Rusty with guarding Deana.

Caitlin tugged on Curtis's sleeve. "Can I tell you something?"

Curtis bent down to look her in the eyes. "What is it?"

"Well… since Mama took on the people who were poor, we're getting picked on at school."

"Helping people is never wrong," Curtis said gently. "You should be proud of the work your mom does."

"I wish the militia kids went to school with us," Caitlin cried.

Rosie and Lenny overheard and exchanged a look. They wondered if Bobbie Sue was having the same issues. They decided not to tell Deana—she already had enough on her plate.

Thinking about her approach with Henry, Rosie decided politeness didn't work. The family would cover the cost of Deana's campaign So, Henry couldn't lord money over her. That seemed to be his key leverage.

"So, we still doing a potluck?" Lenny asked.

"Yes, for our friends. But to bring our campaign to light, I'm thinking a full-on black-tie event at the Country Club."

"Oh, pulling out the big guns, are we?" Lenny cackled.

"Let's start with all the women's groups first, then move on to the Rotary club, the monsoons, the VA. We'll hit them all. I don't want Deana to worry—we'll handle the planning. The holidays are coming up, So, we need as many events as possible."

"Didn't the last junior senator quit and leave the state?" Leroy asked.

"Yes. Why is the question," Rosie said. "We need to find out where he went."

"Tomorrow we'll take a trip to the library for some research," Lenny suggested. "Someone has a snake in the woodpile."

"Good idea," Rosie said. "I'm thinking the board members at the law firm are covering for someone."

Leroy and Rusty nodded. “You may need to be Deana’s security for these events.”

“Does that mean a suit?” Rusty groaned.

“It may, depending on the event.”

“Great. Rusty in a monkey suit. But I can conceal and carry,” he smirked.

“Rosie, can we use Henry for target practice?” Lenny piped up.

“I vote for that,” the boys chimed in.

Rosie smiled. “Pleasant thought, but he’s Deana’s boss. We can’t kill him outright.”

JB announced his presence. “I know Henry has secrets. Folks talk up to a point, then clam up. If I had to guess, I’d say fear of skeletons coming out of the closet.”

Deana agreed, remembering her early conversation with Henry. Many of the town's population had come here to start over after youthful indiscretions that could ruin reputations.

Lenny turned to Deana. "We're going to the local library and Historical Society to learn more about the board members and the 'no mixing' rule."

Normally Deana wouldn't want Lenny to snoop, but in this case, she needed all the information she could get—if only for self-preservation.

"Oh—Lola called. She wants to meet us for lunch."

"Oh Christ," Rosie groaned.

"Rosie, are you ashamed of us?" Deana asked.

"No, Deana Jay. But this woman is a shark in the PR world. She doesn't play fair."

"Neither do we."

"Her questions upset you because you feel we need protection," Rosie said. "Lunch at the club, when Henry is also, expected. Great. They're going to grill you like you're running for junior senator."

"What exactly does she do for the campaign?" Lenny asked.

"If I had to guess," Deana said, "she's a fixer. Her job is to make sure I lead in the polls and am loved by my constituents."

"So, she's looking for dirty laundry," Rosie concluded.

"Yes, she picked apart Curtis. Why did Dean end up in a facility? Why am I called the crusader? Then of course Jake and his family, and finally, my new clients. But the final one was my relationship with the family."

Knowing exactly what that meant, Rosie said, "She's looking for skeletons she can exploit and use to lord over you. And she was rough on Curtis too."

"Sounds like a worthy adversary," Rosie smirked. "It's a basic control tactic, Deana. We've decided the family will cover the cost of your local campaign. The more Henry puts in financially, the more favors he can demand later."

"I understand, Rosie. She didn't seem to accept my National Guard weekends."

"That's because she wants to turn you into a complete Barbie doll," Lenny said, rolling her eyes. "Sounds like someone I'd enjoy torturing."

"We'll handle the town-hall meetings with a potluck to size up how the locals are feeling," Rosie continued. "You need to be seen as someone willing to get your hands dirty, not a prissy witch."

Curtis smirked. "How about a show of Deana's skills that aren't just the law?"

Lenny giggled. "You mean like her expertise with firearms?" "Sort of," Curtis said.

"I'm thinking helping the locals with church events, soup kitchens, etc. Your last event for the local ladies to get fair play worked well. Roland's job, Cloud's new pig, the compensation—this is what matters to small-town folks. A few pictures of her helping the motor-pool guys. Show people she can and will do what it takes. Show the many facets of her skills as a person, not just a lawyer who can run her mouth."

Smiling, Rosie nodded at Curtis in approval.

Leroy cleared his throat. "Keep the kids away from that uppity—well, you know. She'll grill our kids, then find a way to use it against Deana."

Rosie heard the tiny concern in his tone.

Rusty then suggested she keep away from the compound as well. "Pictures of the compound could tip our hand about anonymity."

"Smart, Rusty. Whoever said you don't think was wrong," Rosie smiled.

"She works for Henry and the board of directors. She can't be trusted," Curtis said. "She knows all the political games we aren't aware of. Let her do her job—get Deana elected. The last guy quit, So, they could be seen in office until an election as a temporary solution. But Henry will want Deana in for a full term. He has plans, I'm sure. Committee positions matter."

"Deana, head to work," Rosie said. "Pretend you don't know about our lunch meeting. Let's see how forthcoming he is. Lenny, let's hit the road. Research takes time. Here are full names with addresses to help you."

"The boys scheduled you for concealed-carry permits," Rosie added. "Because of Curtis's guard weekends, you'll need extra security."

"Johnny, how are the ladies doing with their projects?"

"Good, but they need another case of yarn."

"OK, I'll put in another order. What else?"

Johnny pulled out a neatly written list of supplies. Then he asked, "The wives want to know what they should do with the money they've earned."

Rosie smiled. "They may keep it. Put it toward Christmas. We'll start collecting presents for the kids."

Johnny grinned. "Thanks, sis. They work hard—they deserve to spend it."

Deana smiled. “Are we going Soft, Rosie?”

“Never!” Rosie barked. “But if we were, they’ve earned their paycheck. They never complain and they’re always the backbone of our family.”

As everyone parted ways, Deana realized how important a family atmosphere was. Both the militia and the Indigenous community had it—and that was good for everyone. Thinking for a moment, she knew this would be part of her campaign.

Curtis recognized the look in her eyes, usually the one she had right before destroying an opponent in court. Knowing his boss was preparing for a confrontation, he mentally calculated whether he qualified for unemployment.

This probably wouldn’t end well—but not as bad as a family lunch with Henry and Lola. The fallout would be severe.

The drive to town was eerily quiet. At the halfway point, Curtis cleared his throat.

"Boss... what's going on in your head? Lola versus Rosie. Henry will just sit and watch the fireworks. He's setting the fire So, he can watch it burn."

"So, to speak," Deana muttered. "It'll be a pissing contest, and Rosie never loses. Rosie has places I need to address locally—Auxiliary, Rotary Clubs, VA, etc. That's where you find your middle class. Our kind of people. They still believe in government and that hard work gets you through anything."

Walking into the lobby, Curtis said, "Rosie has good practical ideas. Henry can't complain about them."

"Henry complains about anything and everything," Deana said. "Any idea that wasn't his."

"True, boss."

Julie greeted Deana with twenty-five call slips, several headache-inducing callback numbers, but no actual names. Deana looked at one message—the number looked familiar.

"It's about your husband."

Shutting her office door, Curtis sat with his hands folded as Deana called the facility.

"Yes, doctor, I'm returning your call. Has his condition changed?"

"He has made some progress," the doctor said. "Still doesn't recognize the girls, but he does remember Curtis. His mother wants to care for him at home. I tried to explain the volatile outbursts. She even said she'll stop payment on his treatment."

Deana let out a gasp of exasperation. "We pay for him. Has Henry forgotten, or did HR stop the payments from my paycheck?"

"No. But I may need an order of protection to prevent her from pulling him out."

Henry walked in and hit speaker. "I'm Deana's boss. How can I help?"

"Henry," the doctor said, "our issue is Dean's mother wants to bring him home."

"Isn't there a safety issue?" Henry asked. "Without antipsychotics he becomes violent. He still believes the Vietcong are going to kill him. He thinks he's still in the country. He remembers Curtis, but not the girls or Deana. So, you need the court to intervene?"

"Yes. Legally her feelings carry no weight, but she got a lawyer who says Deana abandoned him."

"How? I pay his bills!" Deana cried.

"But you aren't here to visit and support him emotionally."

"He has no idea who I am!"

Henry said, "This should be answered via the appellate court. I'll file a writ, but Deana will have to make an appearance."

Thinking a moment, Henry added, "In lieu of a physical appearance, she can submit her position by written letter. Deana has a full caseload, and I need her here, So, I'll appear for her."

"She is aiming for this Friday to have him released," the doctor warned.

After a few more details, Henry headed back to his office to file on Deana's behalf.

Once he was out of earshot, Deana asked, "What is the real problem?"

“He swings at male orderlies and most female nurses except Nurse Charlotte. She can reach him. If she has a day off, we usually must sedate him and use restraints. The last male nurse went to check on him—Dean was hiding in the dark. He jumped on him, got behind him, put him in a chokehold. After a struggle, other interns restrained him.”

“The nurse went to the ER with broken ribs and a neck injury. This isn’t the first time. He can’t go home with his mother.”

Standing in the hall, Henry had heard what Dean was capable of. This needed to stay out of the press.

Henry filed a notice of appearance for himself and Curtis.

After hanging up, Deana felt her stomach do Somersaults.

Henry knocked Softly. “I’ve filed. Curtis and I will represent your interests.”

Rolling her eyes, Deana asked, “What’s the plan of action?”

“He’s dangerous when not medicated. He has no business outside in the civilized world. He could hurt your daughters, not meaning to. I’ll use Curtis to express the training he had versus Dean. “

“He could go on a spree and be damn near unstoppable. I won’t tarnish his military career, but he’s not functional.”

“Why would you do this, Henry?”

“Because I understand pushy mothers-in-law.”

“No, really, Henry.”

“You need to focus on your campaign. This would look bad in the press.”

"From what I got from the calls I made, your mother-in-law is going to sue you to get money. It has nothing to do with wanting to care for him. Somehow this woman thinks you're wealthy."

"I work for you, Henry. Where am I wealthy?"

Laughing, Henry said, "I can show you your paychecks and how much gets sent to that facility. What is it your daughters say? They call Dean a cabbage-head, correct?"

"I won't even ask how you know that." Curtis looked at Deana, waiting for an answer.

Henry realized the jig was up and needed to tell her. "Lola felt it would be best to meet the family to gauge how much of a problem they'll be during the campaign."

Laughing out loud, Deana said, "Translation: you want to see Lola square off against Rosie?"

"Well, that could be true. But now Curtis and I will be catching a plane in a couple of hours, So, it'll be up to the boys to be your security."

Curtis stood. "Go home and pack a bag."

With a dry tone, Curtis replied, "I always keep a go-bag. You never know where you're going to be sent."

"Always prepared," Henry snickered. "The best Solider is a prepared Solider."

Smiling, Henry added, "I agree."

He then explained he had called Lola to tell her she was on her own. "She's gonna have a hate-on for you, Henry."

"I think Rosie will win," Henry admitted. "I've witnessed her in action.

But because she's such a great strategist, I have a gift for her. I'll give it to her before Curtis and I head out."

As Henry and Deana walked back to his office, Deana became concerned. "Julie and Savannah… what's Henry up to?"

"I'm not sure," Curtis said, "but it has Something to do with the Queen."

Thinking a moment, Curtis added, "What's the best strategy game used for centuries?"

"Not sure."

"It's a military tactic."

Shaking her head, Deana sighed.

Anna squealed, "They're here!"

"Who's here?" Deana asked.

"Your family," Anna growled playfully.

Rosie entered. "Henry would like to see me before the meeting. He told me he and Curtis are going to deal with Dean's mother."

On the way to the conference room, everyone took their seats. Julie announced Henry's arrival.

Henry greeted them. "Gentlemen, how did you fare with your concealed-carry permits?"

Rusty grinned. "Our scores were So, good they couldn't believe it."

Leroy added, "I prefer moving targets."

Henry gulped but tried to smile. "Are you familiar with security procedures?"

"Curtis has trained us," Leroy said.

Henry nodded to Lenny. "I'd like you to go with Deana to events. I'll list you as her aide. I assume you can handle yourself?"

Laughing, Lenny swept Henry's legs out from under him and pointed a handgun at his face. "I think So, Henry. I'll try hard."

Henry just shook his head.

Turning to Deana, he said quietly, "Looks like you have security well in hand."

He placed a flowered print box in front of Rosie. For strategy. Rosie removed the lid and lifted out a three-tiered chessboard with a heart painted on it.

"The Queen of Hearts," Henry said. "Practice strategies."

Rosie smirked. "You could be a worthy opponent, Henry. We shall see."

Standing, she gave Henry a hug and slapped him on the back. "If even a quarter of what Dean's doctor says is true, he can't live outside that facility. And because he doesn't recognize the girls or Deana, he could think they're the enemy."

Curtis interjected, "This woman wants to sue Deana for abandonment, Henry. Is she delusional too?"

"I have no idea," Henry said, "but I'll put a stop to this. Curtis and I need to head out. Please be on your best behavior with Lola."

"Aren't we always?" Woody asked.

Henry rolled his eyes. "I guess it depends on what you consider behaving."

Rusty looked at Henry. "Tread lightly with my old lady. She's feral."

Leroy nodded. "Oh boy."

"Well, ladies," Henry said, "we're headed out."

"Why was Henry worried about our meeting?" Deana asked.

"Because he's seen you in action," Deana cracked.

"We've always been respectful," Lenny giggled.

"Really?" Deana asked. "How about Rosie offering to dog-walk him and make him call her his queen?"

Rosie growled. "It was done in protection. No one gets to threaten Curtis with scrubbing toilets. He's one of us, even though we tease him."

Lenny added, "He'll always be our goof, but truthfully he's been one of us from the start."

"So," Deana said, "are we ready to meet Lola?"

"If she's anything like Henry, this will be fun," Lenny cackled.

Rosie looked at Leroy and Rusty. "You need suits for security detail."

"Don't we get a chance to meet her first?" Leroy asked. "Don't we get lunch?"

"Wine?" Rusty added hopefully.

Leroy laughed. "I brought a stack of hundreds just to instill a touch of humility. Apparently, she has a 98% success rate getting her clients into office. So, let's head to the club."

As they walked, Rosie noticed the fall colors had turned brown under gray skies. "Winters upon us."

Closer to the club, they saw a crowd. Lola was speaking into a microphone, telling the crowd why Deana was the best choice to represent the constituents.

"Here she is—your candidate for junior senator. She will have the ear of the lawmakers."

Greeting everyone with a smile, Deana waved as they were whisked into a private dining room.

After introductions, Lola asked, "Who are those men?"

"My security detail," Deana said. "Curtis and Henry had to go out of town."

After appetizers were ordered, Lola began. "I know why Henry is handling the situation with your husband. I told him it needs to be handled with discretion."

Rosie asked, "Why? Deana has no shame about her husband being sick."

Lola's tone sharpened. "Well, it's not abandonment if you're supporting his stay in the facility. But we don't want constituents to think you just hid him away. It makes you look uncaring. I have it listed as PTSD So, no one questions your motives."

"Now," Lola continued, "let's discuss this family thing. Why are you So, important to our candidate? I want no surprises. No half-answers."

Rosie explained, "I've known Deana since she was a tween. She was a candy striper and met our mother. Once she realized all the kids, she knew where her family, we were all close. Then an accident sent Some of our boys away. The townspeople couldn't get over it. They weren't allowed to homeschool their children because they didn't have college degrees. When a reporter tried to tell the truth about how they were treated, he had an 'accident' and his story never made it to the newspapers. A senator signed off on bombing their mountain— 'send them straight to hell,' he said. All because they wanted to live life on their own terms."

“So, you grew up wanting to protect their rights,” Lola said. “In the UK they’d call you crusaders.”

“‘Crusader’ is Henry’s term,” Deana said. “But yes—protector of the poor. If you look at your bar graphs, you’d see this place is one-sided.”

“The rich treat the working-class poor like garbage. They can’t even control their family size. Birth control costs money. The more Sons you have, the more important you are. Girls are considered a waste—they can’t be sent out to work. They just eat and get pregnant.”

“Now I understand why Henry calls you a crusader,” Lola said. “But now I have to make you appealing to the money-makers.”

“Let’s discuss your campaign plans.”

Rosie cleared her throat. "We do hometown potlucks with town-hall meetings. We can handle the Auxiliary, the Rotary, the VA—small groups. But when it comes to rubber-chicken dinners for donations, that's all you, Lola."

Lola gulped. "Normally we do those dinners for funds."

Deana explained, "When you take their donations, they expect you to side with them on bills."

"Yes," Lola admitted. "But junior senators spend most of their time trying to get funding for projects."

"Like subsidies for farmers," Rosie cackled.

"Exactly," Lola smiled. "I knew you weren't as bad as Henry said."

"Henry isn't used to a strong woman standing toe-to-toe with him," Rosie laughed.

"So," Lola asked, "did you really drop hundreds and say 'money burns'?"

Rosie grinned. "Yes, we did. He was being insufferable."

Laughing hard, Lola said, "You should work with me. That would give Henry a heart palpitation."

Deana explained, "When I was trying to set up my clients' work to be appreciated, I met Henry's wife. She was worse than Henry and made my daughters dislike her. Caitlyn and Bobbie Sue said they wished they had a family like ours So, they wouldn't be So, sad and mean. They didn't understand why she was So, hateful to poor people. Kids understand more than adults."

"Where are those young men going?" Lola asked.

"Suit fitting for security duty."

"Well," Lola said, "since you want to take an active part in this—and because the last junior senator quit—she'll need to be approved fast. Rosie, you and Lenny will handle the small local venues. I'll handle the large groups."

Rosie asked, "Why is Henry backing our girl?"

It seems he has an interest in a few of the committees that would help the board members with their other potential projects. In other words, they need her in place to get things voted for. So, it's not her dedication to the poor; it's for their gratification of the wealthy. Lola has more lists of places to use. There are two state dinners and a few meetings with Some of the congressional aides, to see where she stands on important issues.

"Oh, the old boy network. Deana won't enjoy this. She can handle herself with those blowhards, just So, you know. Other candidates will do a super deep research dive on her and the family."

"So, plan and keep your head down. Oh—and a local radio interview. Also, passing out lists to Rosie and Lenny for the campaign. I will expect a phone call on Henry's results with Dean and his mother."

Rosie and Lenny headed back to the compound to start the campaign work. Deana headed back to the office to check her messages. Henry said they arrived and were headed for the facility to see Dean's doctor. The hearing is tomorrow at 9:00 AM. "We'll call later."

Finishing her phone messages, Deana let out a long sigh. This was going to be a nightmare public health call. They made the rounds for birth control and other medical needs. Marge had called: "Thank you for the public health nurse.

They gave us medicine, vitamins, and iron pills." Rolling also, called, saying Rosie's rocking chair would be ready on Friday.

Also, the girls' cradles for Christmas would be ready the following Friday, a small piece of good news.

Julie knocked softly. "Coffee?"

"Yes, please. Thank you."

While doing paperwork, Deana stared off into space, thinking about Dean's health issues and what the right thing for him truly was. Was she selfish for putting him away? She thought about bringing him home for care, but then she thought about her daughters' safety. If he didn't recognize the girls, he could view them as the enemy. This was all a big mess. Caffeine was not helping this headache.

"I need to go home."

Packing up her briefcase, Deana headed home.

Her arrival home was met with kids screaming, "Hi, Mama!"

"Hello, girls. What did you learn today about the Boston Tea Party?"

"It was interesting. No taxation without representation."

"I guess history class was good today. Mama, can we do a float for the Halloween parade?"

"I think we could do that. You kids draw plans for your float, and I will ask the boys about lumber."

"Uncle Rusty will help," said Bobbie Sue. "And Uncle Leroy will help."

"I'm sure you girls are right. Uncle Leroy always helps us."

"You want Rosie?"

"We wanna build a float for the parade."

"Sounds like fun, girls."

"So, what's bothering you, Deana?" Jade asked.

"Well... it's about Dean."

"All right, let's hear it."

"I feel bad about not bringing him home, but after speaking with his doctor, I think I made the right call. He doesn't recognize me or the girls. What if he viewed us as the enemy?"

"That is a realistic concern. He recognizes Curtis's picture, but I believe it's part of his trauma. Curtis was next to him in-country. They fought side by side. Seems he has a nurse he favors."

"She's the only one he doesn't try to hurt. From what the doctor said, it was Nurse Charlotte's Day off, and the intern came in to check on him. He was sitting in the dark waiting, and he attacked this man along with other staff members. A dose of antipsychotics and restraints were used to calm him down. I don't know what would have happened if Nurse Charlotte ever retired. And now his mother wants to take him home to care for him and sue me for abandonment."

Rosie walked to the tall cupboards, stepping onto the stool. Carefully, she pulled out a strong box. Stepping down, she handed it to Deana.

"Open it, please."

Using a small key, Deana opened the box. Inside were over one hundred receipts of money sent to the facility for Dean's care. Deana then brought out her own collection of receipts from HR proving she—and the firm—were also paying for his care.

Rosie spoke with a stern tone. "Fly was a big portion of Dean's problems. That's why we cover Dean. You make sure he has the best care. That's not abandonment. You care for him whether physically or not. Henry is not going to let her win. It would not help him with your campaign, now, would it?"

Just then the telephone rang, startling both women.

"Hello?"

"It's me. Curtis. We saw Dean today, and he looks healthy, but he has no clue who you are. All he remembers about me is that we were in-country together. We also met with Nurse Charlotte. She has a rapport with him, but each move is slow and with purpose So, he doesn't get alarmed. With lots of help and guidance, he made a birdhouse. They filled it with seeds and hung it on a branch outside his room where he could look through the window and watch the birds. But the Dean we knew is long gone."

"Henry is working on his presentation for the judge," Deana

explained. "We have receipts to prove we paid for Dean's care. Yes, Rosie was kind enough to make copies."

"So, what's Henry thinking?" Curtis asked.

"He has the same expression on his face that he had during Jake's trial."

"That good, huh?" cracked Deana.

"He does love a big challenge. Dean's mom won't know what hit her. The hearing is at 9:00 AM. Henry will be armed with a witness, receipts, and medical reports."

Deana knew Henry would put on a good show, but Dean's mother was another story. She had outlived three husbands and made a lot of money each time one of them died. Men tended to have accidents around her. She was looking at collecting from Deana if Dean went home with her.

"So, it's a money grab," said Rosie.

"Yeah. She's looking for the almighty greenback," Deana said.

"Has she actually seen Dean unmedicated?" asked Rosie.

"Probably not. But his doctor has seen his behavior documented, So, the judge will get a full view of the psychosis—including that poor intern he beat the hell out of because it wasn't Nurse Charlotte. Whatever it is about this nurse, he seems to trust her."

"So, maybe she is the key to describing his problems for the judge," Rosie smiled. "If Henry does his job, it will be a slam dunk."

"Not necessarily," Rosie added. "Mental health law is difficult to wade through. In his case, he has a family member willing to provide care, but the judge will look at the safety issues concerning him in public. Even if the judge agreed to this nonsense, he would start with a halfway house and weekend home visits. They would ease him into it."

"So, how do you really feel about this, D?" Rosie asked.

"I want him to have the best care, but I also, realize he's not mentally stable and needs familiar surroundings and people he trusts. The institution seems to be doing their job, but honestly, the idea that he tried to use tools as weapons is a bit scary. Plus, he didn't know there was anything wrong with it. I had told him to think about the girls. He doesn't recognize them. What if he thought they were the enemy?"

"Sounds like you've made up your mind," Rosie said. "For everyone's safety, he needs to live in the institution."

"Well, at least Lola was receptive to our ideas about the campaign, and she understands about Dean. So, I'm making calls for you to speak at local venues—Auxiliary, Rotary, etc. I figured we'll start off with small places. If no one else runs for that seat, you can be put in temporarily. Then we work on keeping your seat in Congress."

"That would be the fastest way, but I'm sure there's a big macho man Somewhere who wants to be in this position."

"Are you doubting your abilities, Deana Jay?"

"No, I'm not. But let's be honest—these people are of a patriarchal clan. Men are king; women are subservient."

Rusty said, "That won't ever come out of my mouth, but most men are not as enlightened as we are."

"Smart boy," cracked Rosie. "No matter what, everyone counts. No one person is in charge. We vote on actions we take."

"So, what else are we doing?"

"A potluck-type buffet at the club So, you can speak and take questions. Town hall meetings Sound OK, but I'm afraid Lola will be trading favors to get me elected, and I don't like that at all."

Deana started assembling lists of events to attend. Rosie suggested a bubble bath to relax and take her mind off Dean. The kids were asleep. It Sounded like a good idea. The boys had already checked the perimeter, So, all was quiet as Deana stepped into a steamy bath. She sat down, leaning back, closing her eyes. The scent of lavender filled her nose.

Before long, Deana had fallen asleep in the tub, dreaming of Dean threatening to kill her and torture the girls because he believed they were the enemy. Waking, Deana discovered she had slipped under, with only her eyes above the water. Shaking her head, she realized the water was cold and she had been asleep.

Rosie softly said, "I'll call Julie and tell her you aren't coming in. It's obvious you need so, me rest. Now get into bed—that's an order."

Handing Deana warm milk and a cookie, she added, "Now sleep." Rosie's warm milk always had a little additive to help her rest.

As Deana fell asleep, Rosie pulled all the shades to make the room dark for rest. After a late phone call to Julie at home, Rosie finally turned in. As dawn broke, Rosie quietly shut Deana's door and began preparing breakfast for the girls.

"Is Mama sick as fatty Soup?"

"No, dear. Mom is just tired."

"Aunt Rosie, how do you know Mama is tired?"

Laughing, Rosie explained, "She fell asleep in the bathtub."

"Wow, I guess she really is tired. Why do we have to go to all these rallies with Mama?"

"It is important that voters understand that she stands for family values, fair pay for work done, and many other things."

Nodding, the kids knew this was important. As the bus pulled up, a familiar horn beeped. Climbing the stairs, the girls took their seats.

Rosie busied herself with the day's chores. Around 10:00 AM, Deana shuffled into the kitchen.

“What was in that warm milk? I feel like I’ve been kicked in the head by a mule.”

“Coffee,” Rosie smiled. “I called Julie, So, work is covered.”

“I can’t... I can’t take a day off.”

“Look, you were So, tired you fell asleep in the bathtub.”

Nodding in agreement, Deana admitted she had been dragging lately. She looked at the clock, wondering about the hearing.

“Never mind the clock. Eat your breakfast. He’ll call when it’s done. There’s a ladies’ luncheon on Saturday. I think you should attend. Millie and her friends will be there.”

“I see. So, I need to be polite.”

"Hardly. But they do vote, So, it's part of the game. I'm sure Henry told her you were running for office."

"Oh, I'm sure she was just pleased as punch over that."

Laughing out loud, Rosie nodded. "Lenny and I will also, be there."

"Sounds like loads of fun, Rosie. Oh—did you give the orders to the boys to pick up the guns from the armory?"

"Yes. They're taking a couple of younger Guard friends. They'll have the orders hand in hand. I arranged for three for the armory and eleven for us So, it doesn't screw up their count."

"JB has a meeting with Some of the militia connections about artillery, but he needs to be cautious. Let them believe it's all about them while we stock up on supplies. We can plan our first set of strikes, but we cannot declare war. Only

Congress and the President can do that. But there are other methods to achieve our common goal."

"So, ours would be an undeclared war—a police action."

"That's the way a full-on action was done without giving the powers-that-be any information. Lots of guerrilla tactics. Many other countries march in straight lines—no camouflage, no protection. Indigenous tribes won because they didn't conform to our ways of fighting. It's hard to shoot Someone who blends into their surroundings. Think deer hunting—you use tree stands and camo to blend in."

"Sounds like you've thought this out a bit, Rosie."

"It's the only way this is going to work. A full-frontal attack would end with a high mortality rate. We don't tip our hands either. For now, we keep stockpiling supplies. Once I'm elected, I will research what happened, who ordered the attack, and who sent us straight to hell."

"The hardest thing won't surprise you," Rosie continued. "No discussing plans. According to JB and his biker friends, they have stashes of guns and offered us first crack at them."

Nodding, Deana said, "The guns are needed, but proceed with caution. They could be undercover cops."

Rosie became sullen and quiet. "This makes me think of Mind Fly Sally Jean too." A tear slipped down her cheek.

"We are here to avenge the wrong done to us—just for wanting to live by our own rules."

Dressed in workout sweats, Deana asked, "Are you ready for training?"

"Yes, but start out slowly So, you don't mess up your healing."

"Let's start with a walk-run around the track. Now Some calisthenics."

Laughing, Rosie cackled. "Reminds me of high school gym class."

"Light weights for lifting. Now your favorite part—target practice."

"Ah, something I excel at."

After walking the course, Deana smiled. "Now it's time to run the course—only as fast as you're comfortable with." The boys had made a road course with Gators and obstacles.

After completion, Deana told Rosie, "Not bad for someone who's been on their sickbed."

"My skills prove I am still a correct shot. So,, mouthpiece, you want to take the challenge?"

Lenny went to pick up the girls. The whole course, including their version of Victory Tower, was ready.

“Warm up. Stretch. Mark, set, go!”

As Deana made her way through the obstacle course, she headed full-bore to claim Victory Tower, then ran her five miles to complete the practice.

Standing on the porch of the mess hall, Henry stood mesmerized by Deana’s performance. Curtis smiled, knowing Deana could stand her ground with Henry.

Rosie, wiping her neck, beamed. “Did you see our girl?”

“Yes. She is a great athlete,” Curtis said. “You should see the boss hit the heavy bag.”

Henry nodded. “If she handles the heavy bag with the same gusto she uses for concealed carry, I’ll bet on her any day of the week. Most men are intimidated by her skills."

Curtis added, "Well, if she puts this much work in as a junior senator, she'll be on a congressional ticket."

As the compound came into view, Deana recognized Henry and Curtis waiting for her.

"So, how did the hearing go?"

Henry cackled. "They let the judge meet Dean unmedicated. Then they brought him in after his meds kicked in. The judge went through Dean's medical records and ruled as follows: He needs constant medical supervision.

Dean was never abandoned but placed in an institution where he would have 24-hour care. Payments were never missed. Since he doesn't recognize his wife or children, it is in his best interest to remain where he is. The facility is cutting edge. Court adjourned."

"I bet his mom was furious."

"In all honesty, she seemed horrified at his behavior when he wasn't medicated. She withdrew her request to take him home."

"So, how did he look?" Deana asked.

Curtis replied, "Clean and healthy. But he's not home."

Deana became quiet. "So, how did your meeting go with Lola?"

"She got along with Rosie and Lenny well. Here's a list of small venues for our girl to start with. Lola is handling the bigger dinners and such."

As Henry read the list, he noticed Millie's luncheon. "Do you think that's a good idea? Those women are as vicious as sharks."

"I understand, Henry, but if I hide from them, I'm not a good candidate, am I?"

"Agreed, Deana."

As Rosie walked Henry to his car, she explained how tired Deana had been. "I called in for her, So, yell at me if you must, but my concern is for her. I'll tell her to take tomorrow off too. I'll call her after I finalize her list of events."

Looking at Rosie, Henry said, "Jean's mother treated Curtis terribly. He may need a pat on the back. She went So, far as to say Curtis was inferior because he was Black—So, he should be the one who is sick, not her Son."

Lenny quietly listened to all the hateful things being repeated. She whispered to Kay and Bobby as they ran into the mess hall to make Curtis a snack. With Wendy's assistance, they made him an open-faced roast beef sandwich with mashed potatoes and peas. Lenny brought out a four-layer chocolate cake with cream between each layer.

“What’s all this?” Curtis asked.

“We love you, Curtis, no matter what that mean old lady says.”

Tears filled Curtis’s eyes. He knew they truly meant it. Lenny jumped on him, and Curtis rubbed the top of her head.

“Curtis, you are family—even if you were purple or green. So, go ahead, Lenny, I know you’re dying to say it.”

“We love you. You’re good.”

Laughing and crying at the same time, Curtis cracked, “I love you too, you white-bread ditch.”

Shaking his head, Leroy asked, “Why are we giving the family love speech?”

Lenny replied, “Seems Deana’s mother is prejudiced against Curtis.”

Rusty said, “Why? Curtis is cool.”

"The girls told us she is mean. Mean, mean."

"I understand. Do we have to like her?"

Rosie gently said, "We pray for people like your grandmother, because ignorance is not OK. You girls understand?"

They hugged Curtis. "No matter what, Curtis—we love you."

A faint smile crept across Curtis's face. He knew they meant it. But he also, knew that with just as much hate, some people would toss you out of the family—maybe with a small 'accident' to remind you of your place in the hierarchy.

JB and the boys were out on the gun run, but they had already been warned to be cautious. Being the newbies, the locals might be looking for a way to "make their bones," So, to speak.

Do not start conversations about weapons. Watch who initiates that conversation—they are either a top lieutenant or even the president of their group.

Going over the list of functions, Deana realized she would need a different speech for each. She also, found herself thinking how awful Henry's wife must be, for Henry to warn her. With each meeting, Deana would hear many different opinions on what the state needed for its people.

Rosie showed Deana a food and seating chart.

"Curtis is back. Won't he be my security?"

"Yes, but our boys will also, be in place, just in case. I understand Lola's idea about the girls, but that can also, put a target on their backs. So, extra personnel when the girls travel with you.

But I do agree with you about ulterior motives. As far as Henry goes, handshake promises for contracts or contributions to the campaign... he then complained. That's why we should cover the financial part of the campaign—spreading out the power spectrum."

Deana asked, "Yes, the less control Henry has, the better for us?"

"Exactly," replied Rosie.

"Well, you don't have to go to the office tomorrow, So, you can work on your speech. Lola wants to submit reasons for me to cover this position as a temporary option, So, when there's an acknowledged campaign, they can look at my track record."

Rosie smiled. "That would make things much easier."

"But Rosie, that's not a challenge," whined Deana.

"No—the challenge is keeping the position permanently, not temporarily. Think of it as being dropped behind enemy lines and having to survive. That's why temporary."

"So, you agree with Lola about the temporary position?"

"Deana, we need to get you into a position where you have access to the Old Boy Network. They'll get comfortable around you and let their guard down, So, snooping won't be So, obvious. But for the campaign, we will still speak at the used venues because they're local folks—proving you're still one of them, someone to be counted on by her constituents, not sitting on the sidelines."

"I'd like to discuss Curtis with you."

"All right."

"Dean's mother said horrible things to him. Lenny and the girls tried to make him feel loved, but it's obvious it hurt his pride."

"She has always felt that way," Rosie said. "She's from the old South, So, her beliefs are that anyone not of her descent is unworthy in her view. I've been in screaming matches with her because she is a condescending, overbearing witch with a 'the world owes me' mentality—courtesy of Dean and others—more times than I can count. But in this case, I'm glad Henry handled her, because I'd have been in jail."

Rosie smiled. "I will give Henry the acknowledgements he deserves for the way he handled Dean's case. I bet the look on her face was priceless."

"Since you saw Dean unmedicated and out of control, Rosie, I have to stand by my decision to keep him there. He might not mean to hurt the girls, but I can't take that chance."

Hugging Deana, Rosie whispered, "You need to do what's best for the whole family, not just a select few. This is why you were chosen to lead us. You have the heart of a warrior, the mind of a great general, and the So,ul of a queen. Nana would be pleased at how far you've come. The boys will take turns walking the perimeter. You know this is just a passing contest to see if they can scare you off the campaign trail."

"So, did the guys get their suits?"

"You wait—they look the part."

Just then Rusty walked in—dark blue suit, white shirt, black shades.

"Wow, Rusty, you look all right cleaned up," smiled Deana.

Leroy came in to donning his new suit.

"Very nice, guys."

"Do we have to wear the damn tie? It makes me feel choked."

"So, where are you hiding those handguns, boys?"

"Right here under our jackets—plus ankle holsters. We are prepared."

Lenny, dressed in a pantsuit with a Glock in her waistband, said, "No—just put your hair up So, it doesn't get in the way of watching the crowd."

Next came the kids dressing. Rosie smiled. "I see them in their dress cadet uniforms." Curtis was in his dress uniform too, full of ribbons and brass.

"So, Dee, what do you think you're going to be wearing for these speeches?" asked Lenny.

"Depending on who I'm addressing—either full dress uniform or a suit. Town hall meetings mean my best flannel and jeans."

"So, what was Lola talking about?"

"Seems Henry and Lola can write up an explanation of why I have the credentials to be put in this spot temporarily until next year's election. If that happens, then the campaign will be to keep me in the position."

"So, you have a few options. We'll know more at our next meeting with Lola."

Curtis announced that Henry seemed to enjoy his court appearance and shutting down Dean's mom.

"I hate to admit it," Curtis said, "but Henry is a hell of a trial lawyer. He literally got her into a trap and then closed off the exit. She didn't know what hit her. I introduced Henry to our old boys and our old boss. He was duly impressed. Henry bragged about you—Triple Crown. Then over Jake and his family. He smiled and said there was pride on his face, like a dad when his child scores in a baseball game."

"Not much talk in town about the mountain getting blown up."

"So, no one asked about us?" asked Rosie.

"Nope. Seems we didn't leave a lasting impression—but we will this time around. I went to the newspaper and got you guys a copy of his obituary, but his boss had a file meant for Deana to have for safekeeping."

Rosie thought for a moment, then cleared her throat. "We will show the file to the newest members of our collection of family. Then they'll understand why we feel the way we do and why we're ready to stand our ground against dirty, tyrannical politicians."

Deana's part quieted the room. "But remember—a governor could not make that decision. Senators make such decisions; governors just carry them out. So, the term 'send them straight to hell' had more fire behind it than we knew. But since I have tomorrow off, I guess we will start working on posters and lining up speaking engagements."

Rosie looked Deana in the eye. "You need sleep. Sleep in. You need rest or you won't be any good to anyone. You're stretched too thin."

Rusty spoke. "Let's electrify the fence. Those idiots from town will learn not to be out here on your property."

"You need to be careful with the wattage. We have kids and animals," replied Deana.

"Understood," Rusty said, though his thoughts went directly to teaching those old boys their place.

Leroy asked, “Hey Rosie, what is Henry up to with that gift?”

“Well, from what I understand, a three-dimensional chessboard teaches strategy—how to win against an opponent. It also teaches patience, strikes, and blocks. So, yes, it’s a fancy strategic game. I believe he wants to test my skills as a leader.”

“Are you sure he’s not looking for Some other advantage?”

“That maybe. But I believe this is a test to see how far in we will allow him.”

“I thought Henry didn’t approve of us,” Leroy said.

“I believe we are interesting to him. Henry is used to having total control in every aspect of his life. He’s already figured out he has no control over Deana, So, he figures if he gets friendly with me, he'll regain control. Henry has never figured out that Deana doesn't take orders from anyone but me—and sometimes not even then."

"What happens if Henry is like us?"

"You mean skeletons in the closet?"

"Yes," said Leroy.

Deana explained, "Henry said many people moved to Montana to start over with a clean slate. 'Youthful indiscretions,' I believe he called them. So, the town that believes in no mixing has secrets."

"All right, time to head out, boys. Morning comes early."

Giving Rusty and Leroy a hug, Deana thanked them.

"Lenny, I know dressing like this is Something you don't like, but thank you."

"It's fine, Dee. But I would worry about our buddy Curtis—his feelings were really hurt."

Nodding, Deana said, "I will speak with him. He'll be fine. Wendy's hug was genuine—her love was real."

While Rosie was outside saying goodbye, Deana spoke a thought aloud. "And So, it begins."

Standing behind her, Curtis said, "I guess it's starting."

"I guess So, Curtis... you, OK? Lenny is concerned about you."

Laughing softly, he said, "As strange as this Sounds, I felt almost confident in the love from these crazy-ass family members. They don't judge me for my skin color, medals, or anything else. I'm judged by what I bring to the friendship."

Standing outside, Rosie whispered to JB, "He's ours. And he will be a great leader for Soldiers—whether in battle or in Solidarity."

JB looked into Rosie's brown eyes. "The bikers are willing to join because we believe in living life on our own terms. Each group has their own reasons for joining, but they all agree with the manifesto on how we live together."

Smiling a sad smile, Rosie said, "We'll talk tomorrow."

"Goodnight."

Curtis headed to his place for Some much-needed sleep. Deana, in her pumpkin PJs, got under the covers. Sleep came almost immediately. Rosie headed for her room, peeking in on the kids and Deana before pouring herself into bed.

Deana dreamed of taking the podium with a crowd full of men like Jake screaming she had no right to be there.

"Your job is to take care of the house and the family! Women are to be subservient to all men!"

Deana woke up in a full sweat. She sat up, startled and shaking. Rosie quietly opened her door.

"Bad dream?"

"Oh God, yes—it was horrible."

After Deana explained her nightmare, Rosie said, "Sounds like a fear resurfacing in your mind. I believe your fear was justified. Since his death, you don't have to face that anymore. Don't worry, Deana. You're afraid of the unknown. Once you committed to running for office, you agreed to deal with the unknown. And just because people agree with our manifesto doesn't mean they'll fight when it finally happens."

Smiling, Rosie cooed, "It's the uncertainty of what comes next. Good thing, Henry gave you the day off. Back to bed with you."

As Rosie shut Deana's door, she began thinking of the best way to handle her concerns.

Knowing she wouldn't fall back asleep, Rosie made coffee and worked on lists. Lists always comforted Deana's logical brain. As the girls woke, Rosie shushed them.

"Mama is still asleep. She had a bad dream, So, we'll let her sleep in."

Bobbie Sue took her bear into Deana's room and tucked it under her mother's arm. Rosie smiled as she watched Bobbie Sue give Mama her bear for comfort.

"Aunt Rosie, why oatmeal?"

"Because it's warm and filling on a cold morning."

"I guess you're right, Aunt Rosie."

"I am always right," cracked Rosie. "Eat. There's the bus, girls."

After a few minutes of thinking, Rosie called Henry.

"Hello, do you know who this is?"

"Of course, I know who you are. What's going on this fine morning?"

"Concerned about the chances our girl will be put into that position temporarily."

"Lola and I are writing a presentation for the powers that be on her qualifications. That way she'll have a chance to prove herself before the real campaign. The only people who might balk would be Jake's buddies, but most of the town is pleased with how she handled

Jake and his family. I foresee her clients coming out in force to support her."

"OK, I see. Circumventing the campaign and going for the temporary slot—no rubber-chicken dinners to gag through. Straight to the heart of the matter. Fastest way to get her in position. Why do you care, Henry?"

"Our girl has shown a fierce loyalty this town hasn't seen in years. They deserve someone to fight for them. Heaven knows they've been treated poorly for many years by the money makers."

"So, we treat this as planned until Lola and I finish our presentation, with a letter of accolades from her previous employer along with her National Guard awards. The idea is to show she can handle many committees because of her experience."

Nodding as if Henry could see her, Rosie said, "I want to trust you, Henry. Do not make me regret this trust."

Smirking, Henry replied, "I've seen enough of your family to know I don't want to disappoint them."

Rosie cackled. "You're learning, Henry. There might be hope for you yet."

"Geez, thanks, Rosie."

"Before you know it, Henry, you'll love us just like Curtis does."

"Honestly, Rosie, I don't believe I had a choice."

Hanging up, Rosie realized Henry might be an ally—whether he wanted to be or not.

Making notes on her list, Lenny came bouncing through the door with the enthusiasm of a baby lioness.

"Where are the boys?"

"They're coming. And it seems Henry and Lola are doing a presentation to the bigwigs to get Deana in as a temporary junior slot. Then all she has to do is keep the position. He even mentioned a letter of accolades, ribbons, awards from the Guard, and of course her Triple Crown with Jake."

"So, Henry's on our side?" Lenny asked.

"I think he wants to align himself with a winning team."

"So, what's the play?" Rusty asked.

"We plan for events like Saturday's ladies' luncheon. If anything changes, Lola will tell us."

"Where's D anyway?"

"She had a bad dream last night, So, she's still sleeping. We can keep the plans going. Everything went fine with the trips to the armories—small amounts seemed to work. While I spoke with JB last night, it seems we have interest from the biker community. They also, believe in living life on their own terms. So, we have several factions interested, but I'd like to make copies of the reporter's file So, each leader understands we were truthful in our manifesto and persecuted for how we live."

"Please set a meeting with the leaders. Transparency is necessary for trust between factions," Rosie said.

Lenny smirked. "Maybe we should show it to Henry. He always said he understands our crusader role—but limited, right?"

"Depending on his reaction," Rosie replied. "You boys handle the leaders with this information."

"Lenny, it's time to visit Deana's clients from the tractor path. See if they need help acquiring more supplies for their work."

Understanding their assignments, each left in different directions.

"JB, I'd like you to start sharing this with your group So, they understand the real reason we feel the way we do about those SOBs who destroyed our mountains."

"Are you sure you want me to do this?"

"Yes. It's the only true way to gauge their dedication to our cause."

"Won't that open us up to problems?"

"Not necessarily. We'll show it only to those we feel can handle it. Some won't."

After listening to the kitchen conversation, Deana realized Rosie was preparing the manifesto members for a new regime.

"It's time for us to bring our views to light. Those who agree will fall in line. Those who don't will fall by the wayside."

"Geez, Rosie, why don't you just ask for a blood oath?" cracked Deana.

"Don't laugh—that's a good idea."

"That's a bit extreme, isn't it?" Deana cried.

"Well, since I heard everything... you on Henry's side now?"

"I think he's more like us than we thought. So, —you need a speech for Saturday's luncheon?"

"Well, how about I open it up for questions? Those ladies will be hard to win over. Men are supposed to be in politics while ladies keep a perfect home."

Deana shook her head. "It's like a throwback to the '50s, '60s, and '70s.

Home and Garden on everyone's coffee table. That's why I'm a threat to these women and their way of life."

"You are a triple threat. You're a mom, you're a lawyer, and you're a ranking military officer. Those women are scared to death they'll be expected to work the way you do. Plus, you're a crack shot."

"Stop blowing smoke up my ass, Rosie. I know what I am. I also, know my go-getter attitude is a problem for Some people. I'm here to do my job and lead us to victory."

"Sounds like you're back among the living. Let's start with my lists."

"Rosie, can I have coffee first?"

"Eggs Benedict and coffee. Miss 'I'm inviting Henry.'"

"Why? Do I want to see him on my day off?"

“This is to see his reaction to the reporter’s file. Testing Henry’s resolve. The boys are doing the same as the other leaders. Feeling people out is a must.”

Nodding, Deana said, “Like vetting a witness to make sure their position doesn’t change. So, I’m making an appearance?”

“No. You stay here. Work on your speech or Q&A.”

Putting on a plaid skirt with boots and a corduroy blazer with a slate-colored shirt, folder in hand, Rosie went to the club to meet Henry. Walking with purpose, she knew she had to extend the olive branch.

As Rosie was seated, she could feel the stares in her direction. Henry joined her with a greeting.

“So, you have Something for me to read?”

"It will enlighten you as to why we feel as we do. I ordered you a martini and the lunch special."

Surprised at being on the receiving end of hospitality, Henry chuckled. "So, this is how it feels to be on the other foot."

Rosie smiled. "I am an equal-opportunity hostess."

He ate and read, trying to digest what he saw. Clearing his throat, Henry began:

"So, according to this file, you were singled out because of how you choose to live."

"Yes, Henry. We lost many family members that day on the mountain. When this young man refused to stay silent, he had an 'accident.' Convenient, isn't it? This is where Crusader came from."

"After we lost Ma and Sally Jean, it was only a matter of time before they took aim at us. A senator gave the go-ahead to the governor: 'Send them straight to hell.' But we knew it was coming. So, I bought land and started our compound here in Montana."

"I see. So, this is sanctuary."

"Yes. And I will make sure it stays that way."

"This explains many things about our Crusader. So, how does Curtis fit into all of this?"

"Curtis and Dean were best friends—same unit, in-country together. They arrived at Deana's law school graduation together. They were family. But when they came home, Dean wasn't the same. PTSD, drinking, drugs. He couldn't be trusted with the girls."

"He was violent, and only Curtis could handle him. Dean was in a bar and Fly spiked his drink with LSD, sending him into psychosis. He thought Charlie was trying to kill him. The hospital evaluated him and suggested a long-term facility. After Some work, we found him a good one, and we've been helping cover the cost."

Henry asked gently, "One of the family dosed him?"

"It doesn't matter. He is getting better now. You... you are family now, Henry. The playing field is even."

Ordering another drink, Henry asked, "OK, I know about Fly. But how in the hell did you get So, many people here? Come on, Rosie. How did that happen?"

"Henry, you're smart. What never gets stopped by DOT?"

Thinking for a moment— "Ah, shit. A school bus."

"When he was in charge of getting the compound ready for our arrival."

"Now that makes sense. No one knows you're here. So, are you going to kill me off?"

"Of course not, Henry."

Rosie looked into his eyes with a realistic sense of equality.

"So, there it is—the truth. Can you be trusted to deal with this?"

Henry smiled. "This is why I got you a special gift. You will be a worthy adversary in a test match. And so, our friendship begins. Since we're sharing, I brought you the rough draft of our presentation. Read it carefully."

Rosie pulled out a red pencil, underlining things to be changed.

The appearance of Rusty and Leroy in suits startled Henry.

"You look nice, boys," Henry smiled.

"We got pictures for our security badges."

Henry cracked, "You boys look FBI-worthy."

Rusty grumbled, "I hate ties."

Smiling, Rosie told her brothers how handsome they were when they cleaned up. Looking down at the pages, Rusty cracked, "I see she brought her red pencil."

Nodding in compliance, he knew he was about to get harassed and learn things in family style.

As the boys left, they told Henry, "Good luck."

Henry turned to Rosie

"What else should I know about, or what should we discuss?"

"Our girl will address your wife's luncheon, So, maybe you could speak with your wife."

"All right... why?"

"Your wife upset Deana's daughters. They said she was a mean lady, and that if she had a family like ours, she wouldn't need to be So, sad and so, mean. I didn't realize she was So, rude to Deana. She also feels that Curtis is not worthy because of his race. I know you guys have a 'no mixing' policy, but he is family to us. So, you will need to get her in line—otherwise I will let her meet, Lenny."

Henry straightened. "OK, all right. I will handle my household, and you handle Deana."

"You know no one handles her. Mom showed her what family should be, and that's what she strives for. Anything else you care to criticize about my family?

I assume your wife was born into money—that's why she feels entitled."

"Yes. Her father was on the board of directors, just like me. And I was considered unworthy by many to marry his princess. So, yes, I do understand."

"So, now you understand what transpired?"

"Yes. Everything. But who dosed Dean?"

"Fly. He has passed since then, So, we helped cover the cost. Truthfully, I felt you could handle the history we shared. The reporter was going to tell the truth about how we were treated. When he refused to cave, they arranged an 'accident.'"

"You came here to start over?"

"From what I understand—yes."

"Now let's get to it. Do you believe you can get her into office temporarily?"

Thinking a moment, Henry replied, "Yes. Deana is qualified, and they need the seat filled ASAP."

"Does the board want a backyard girl?"

"Yes, but they're interested in a few committees—like subsidies for farms, health care clinics for county folks. Plus, they want to remove guns. That troubles us. Montana is pro-gun. Many folks hunt for food. Deer are a major food Source here. Gun control is a Sore subject for most of our constituents. And of course—tax breaks for those who make six figures."

"Lola has Some charts for our Crusader to familiarize herself with." He handed the packet to Rosie. "I need to get back to the office, but we'll talk again."

When he returned to pay the bill, the waitress said it had already been taken care of. Turning to Rosie, he tipped his hat with a quiet "Thank you" as she walked toward the front of the country club.

Tears filled her eyes as she thought of the brave reporter, Tim Daly, who tried to tell the truth about a tyrannical governor who wanted to "send us straight to hell." Touching her scars, she knew it wouldn't be the last gunshot she would feel.

Lenny jumped out of the car. "Rose, are you OK?"

"Yes. Just reminded me of our trials—just trying to live free on our own terms."

"What's in the packet?" Lenny asked.

"Charts from Lola So, Deana can familiarize herself with the new results. Henry feels she has a high chance of taking the temporary spot. Then it's just a matter of keeping it."

Pulling in, Lenny noticed Deana sitting outside with a drink and a cigarette.

"Since when did you go back to smoking?"

"I spent time with Lola. Henry sent this packet home with me. It's charts on the locals—what they need, who needs what. My job is to figure out what I can offer these people. I can't promise things I can't deliver. The Old Boy Network has Shawnee Town full of fear that I'm here and that I treat everyone fairly. My new clients are thrilled with me. Now—how do I get the rich people to need me?"

Rosie growled, "How many have you had?"

"This is my first one, honest, Rosie."

"So, did you give Henry our history?"

"He read the file the reporter Tim Daly put together."

Rosie admitted she thought Henry's reaction would have been wilder, but he was conservative with his answers. "But he now knows what kind of stock our girl comes from. She won't quit. Henry has secrets himself. I don't believe he was born with a silver spoon like his wife. So, his views on class are different."

"Are you prepared for the luncheon on Saturday?"

"Yes. I believe my girls should wear their cadet uniforms, and I will also, be in full dress uniform."

Lenny spoke. "D, you're showing that the girls are just as strong when it comes to a fight. But you need those uniforms adorned with their ribbons and awards. I assume the same applies to yours—and Curtis's."

Nodding, Rosie said, "They will be ready."

"How's your speech coming?"

"Well, it's time for Henry's wife and the other women to have bigger roles than just being housewives."

"Geez, Deana, are you going to go for the jugular at the luncheon?"

"Why not? I am just as good with a gun or rifle as any man. But that's not what they think a woman should be."

"Well, you are nothing if not an unusual woman."

"Are you going to let the girls talk?"

Smiling, Deana said, "Yes. I want them to talk about teamwork—working for the betterment of your team. Never leave a man behind. Never kill animals except for food. Then I will talk about how important family and community are—and communication."

"Sounds like you have plans."

"No—just an awakening for the ladies of this town."

"What about Curtis?"

"I'd like him to talk about life in-country. You literally put your life in your hands, and they put their life in yours. These ladies have been sheltered from politics, but they have votes too—not just the men."

"Sounds like you're ready for a throwdown," cackled Lenny.

"Unfortunately, these ladies haven't been brought into the political arena. But these charts will get their attention. Money increases make the shopkeepers happy and keep them busy."

"Did Lola explain about using the temporary appointment to take the position, then just keeping the seat?"

A small smile tugged at Deana's lips. "Henry is pushing So, hard—he must have committees he wants me to have access to."

Lenny growled, “Just to better his position. He is a snake.”

Rosie added, “But he seems to understand our history. He didn’t blink. Maybe he has skeletons in his closet.”

Rosie then took Deana’s pack of cigarettes. “No more of these. You can’t have vices—they will use it against you. These witches will pick you apart. Remember that.”

Always the proper lady, Deana, acknowledged that she and Curtis might get hit with questions about Dean.

“Sounds like you’re expecting a storm,” Rosie said.

“I’ve learned it’s better to be over-prepared than underprepared. Society vipers don’t play fair. So, I am prepared.”

“So, will Henry show up? Or Lola?”

"Not sure, Mama."

"Here's our part to talk about," Rosie said as she read. Deana teared up.

"Hi, I am Kaylin, and I am Bobbie Sue. We are new to your school. We joined cadets to learn team building, proper gun safety, putting up a tent, making a fire, etc. Other kids who joined cadets learn self-reliance. Coming from our large family, we learn to work as a team for the betterment of all of us. We learn to cook what we can find. Perimeter checks..."

Kaylin spoke, "I love and respect my mom—not just because she's a lawyer or a Soldier, but because she protects her clients and anyone else who needs help."

Bobbie Sue said, "I will share my mom with people because she's a wonderful mom."

Deana whispered, "I love you girls So, much."

"Can we say we love Curtis too?"

Thinking a moment, Deana exploded with, "Yes! I would expect that. Curtis is a great man and a great Soldier—and my best friend."

Curtis cracked, "You say that shit and you won't get that seat."

"That's bullshit. I will not allow them to talk down to you."

JB came in with a nod to Rosie, speaking privately.

"So, how did your brethren react?"

"Willing to help with the firearms and planting small explosions to keep them chasing their tails."

"So, they're on board?" Rosie asked.

"Well, they believe in living life on their own terms. I also, let the president of the club read the file. Then he read it out loud."

"How about the Indigenous Indians?"

"They understand. They seem ready for a fight—willing to teach how to blend in with surroundings."

"What about the militia?"

"They also, read the file. I explained what the reporter was going to publish—which got him killed."

"OK. What about the locals?"

"At first, they didn't want to get involved. Until they read that file. Now we have interested men."

"Once Deana takes the seat, she can access files," Rosie said. She admitted she wanted to get up close and personal with that governor.

Laughing heartily, JB said, "I would not want to be him."

"You would be correct in assuming I will make it hurt before he begs for death."

"Next—we need a map of Montana to plan small strategic strikes with large spaces in between So, police and personnel will be spread thin."

"Good news then. So, we take over without suspicion."

"I want you to split up attacks by grid. For electricity—it's hard to fight when you can't see. The term 'war' has ugly connotations. 'Undeclared war' or 'police action' seems more palatable to locals."

As Curtis listened, standing behind the wood pile, he knew his prayers went unanswered. War would happen. With any luck, the body count would be small.

With all the problems in Waco and Ruby Ridge, Curtis knew it could blow up badly. As he watched, he realized he might not have much time left. Hopefully the holidays stayed relatively calm—but that would be the ideal time for small strikes.

Rosie suggested a Saturday evening meeting to lay out plans—what they still needed to acquire.

“We need to keep Deana away from the actual strikes. She needs total deniability. At least for a while,” Rosie said. “We need her making posters and potlucks to keep her pure with the poor folks. The older kids will learn triage, bandaging, and rolling bandage.

“We will need Some basic medical supplies. Lessons on CPR will also, be necessary. Bulk supplies will be noticed, So, maybe Gilbert can help. I’ll give him a call.”

“Who?” Deana asked drowsily.

“So, what’s next?”

"Let's just get through Saturday's lunch and then plan the next event."

"You OK to go back to work, Deana?"

"Yes, Rosie, but I don't like bureaucracy BS. Still, I'll do what it takes to get elected."

"Will you need Rusty and Leroy Saturday?"

"Yes—to keep everything professional. Those ladies will be watching, and we're not giving them any excuse."

"Have you worked on the Q&A part of this?"

"I've memorized the data from Lola's graphs. The girls are ready to discuss how much they've learned. And Henry seems to believe they can get me the spot temporarily, which means Something could go wrong without needing to run a full campaign."

Thinking a moment, Rosie said, “I’d say there are backroom deals being made. To keep it honest, we should invite your clients to join us.”

Laughing, Deana said, “Oh shoot—Millie will have a cow.”

“Probably true,” Lenny cackled, “but I intend to keep it a fair playing field.”

“Well, I’ll be there to fix ruffled feathers,” Rosie cooed. “I’ll call for extra tables. Don’t forget the militia wives’ invite.”

“Trying to start a fight?” Deana asked.

“No—but all women have concerns. Showing that all women feel the same will help with community relations. Men are also, judgmental, So, I need to show it’ll be tough on the issues. Let the battle cries ring.”

“Heading to work, boss,” Curtis said.

"Yes, Curtis. This is the beginning of the pre-battle. We're watching to see who aligns with our views. I hear Henry is doing a few meetings himself to feel out the male population."

"OK, So, I'll ask."

Pulling into the associate parking lot, Deana knew it would be a long few days before her official campaign speech. Heading to her office, she was met with a stack of messages. Sitting down, she began Sorting through them.

Rosie handled the extra tables. Lenny visited both clients and militia wives, inviting them to the luncheon. Each agreed to come.

"Savannah, I need instructions for the messages. And I'd like to call Olive and Edith to extend invitations."

Using the conference room, Deana began putting up all the charts—pie charts, bar graphs—showing which areas needed extra attention. Employment numbers were 5% better since Deana used common sense to Solve issues between neighbors.

Public health nurses reported an upturn in local sales. Even the local church noticed an increase in parishioners. Halloween was shaping up to be a fun event for the children's parade.

As Deana took notes for her speech, she muttered, "This town lacks pride in its people—just money."

Quietly, Curtis snuck up behind her and touched her shoulder. Deana spun, ready to throw a roundhouse kick, and Curtis caught her leg before it hit his face.

Laughing, Curtis said, "Too slow."

"Would you care to find out?"

"Nah, boss. That's all right."

"With all these charts, it looks like you're planning an operational meeting."

"Once we try the first couple of events, I can tailor my speech and Q&A to their concerns. It seems the furniture factory needs to put on a third shift—they have several back orders. I guess our idea is keeping the factory afloat."

"Oh yeah—Mama, I was told to give you this note."

We would like to thank you for getting us the proper amount for our handmade items. We even made enough money to buy Christmas gifts for the children, and our store is holding a beautiful tool chest on wheels full of tools. I am So, excited. I have never made enough to do this. Would Curtis help me get it home?

Smiling, Deana said, "I'll send Rusty and Leroy. They'll move it for you and give your ideas on what else goes with the tools."

Curtis giggled. "Seems like you're popular."

"Well, I treat all people the same. That's all they want—fair treatment."

Henry stood quietly in the doorway, listening to Deana brag about her clients.

"Sounds like you've scored big with the locals," he snorted.

Clearing her throat, Deana said, "They're pleased with their sales. They even made enough to buy a tool chest with new tools—and it's on wheels. But Henry, it's almost Halloween, not Christmas. When you have very little income, you start months early. I remember waiting for the Christmas catalog as a kid and marking all the pages."

"Sounds like your clients are pleased with their representation."

"Actually, all they want is to be treated fairly. Shopkeepers weren't being fair. Just because you have money doesn't mean you have empathy, compassion, or common decency."

"Always the Crusader," Henry muttered.

"Be careful, Henry. You created this persona, but it could come back to bite you in the butt. And don't forget—I'm still your employee."

"Oh, Deana, you'd never let me forget that you're my subordinate."

"So, since we're talking honestly—why are you really supporting me for public office?"

"There are several committees that could use your fire and spirit."

"And it's a money-making opportunity for the law firm."

"That too. If we get you in temporarily, then you just must keep the seat."

"So, you're still going to speak at Millie's luncheon?"

"Yes, Henry. And yes—both my daughters will speak. Curtis will also be present for the Q&A in case they have questions about his military career. Rusty, Leroy, and Lenny will be security."

Henry complained, "They look like agents."

Deana chuckled. "To know your enemy, you must learn from them. The boys will get a giggle out of that."

Shaking his head, Henry said, "Could you please not demonstrate your prowess with firearms?"

Going back to the charts, Deana knew she'd have to explain what the graphs meant—otherwise they wouldn't understand the demographics.

Savannah popped her head around the corner. "Can I get you Something?"

"No, but I need to make booklets to pass out. It needs to explain our dream, our demographics, and what it means for the town."

"Should it be... dumbed down?"

"I wouldn't say dumbed down—just easily understood. Pictures help."

"Rosie is planning to be there."

"I assumed So,."

"I'll set them up and send them to print. Should I send your dress uniform to be cleaned? There are more ribbons and awards to add."

"Do you think Henry will show up?"

"He's afraid you'll get into it with Millie. But you'll keep your composure. Emergencies or immediate cases have been sent to mediation."

"Good. Less time in court."

"My average. Lola will be in to see how preparations are coming."

"Will do," Deana smiled.

Lola called. "Deana, can we change our meeting to a lunch meeting?"

"Yes. Is there a problem?"

"No. But after the luncheon, you may be vetted."

"Vetted? You mean questioned."

"Yes."

"So, why are they starting this part So, early?"

"Because the position needs to be filled."

"What's on deck with the committees?"

"Taxes on alcohol, take-out assistance for poor families, cuts to health care—just to name a few."

"Well, alcohol tax is a yes. Those taxes can help our schools with advanced classes and sports teams. You'd be surprised how a town comes together to support local teams. Assistance should help with school laundry. Full bellies make kids healthier and more intuitive in class."

"As for health care, it's bare minimum for families. Immunizations aren't covered, So, health clinics at the school help. They also have life issues. We need to do better for our children. They will carry on after we're gone. They need skills to prosper—not depend on a system that failed them."

"Wow. Now I understand the term 'Crusader.' The passion you carry for your people—and the townspeople. That is why I believe you belong in Montana politics."

"Even though I'm female?"

"That is part of it. I'll see you at noon at the Country Club."

Savannah said, "Sounds like a great speech. It will be a great race."

"I think Lola recorded my rant to play for all those old men."

"Here's our booklet for the luncheon for you to check before I send it to the printers."

Reviewing each page from top to bottom, Deana said, "No mistakes. Especially with the special ladies of Society attending. Once they're printed, leave one for each board member. No surprises. Save one for Lola."

Packing up completed files, Deana designed a waiting room that could become an office if she ran out of space.

"Three jobs. Why the hell am I doing this to myself?"

After giving security their orders, Deana headed out to meet Lola. The air was crisp with a cold bite; her toes tingled as she approached the club. She had a feeling she couldn't shake—not anxiety or fear, but a calm mind. She knew this was her path to protect the townsfolk.

Lifting her frozen feet up each step was difficult. As she opened the huge wooden door, a blast of warm air hit her from the vent overhead. The waitress showed Deana to her table.

"Anything to drink, ma'am?"

"Yes. Coffee."

While looking at the menu, Deana felt a cold presence behind her. Turning slowly, she realized it was Rosie.

"Surprised to see you. Let me guess—Lola called you?"

"Yes. I got to listen to your views on the town issues, and it was very Sound advice. I assume it will be played for the gentlemen who will vet you."

Deana cracked a smile.

"What are you giggling for?" Rosie asked.

"Henry thinks the boys look like agents."

"Oh look—no wind or Rusty. That means you can go undercover."

"Stop it," Rusty complained.

Leroy glowed, saying he was proud of how he looked. Lola smiled and pinched his cheek.

"Are we all here?"

"Yes—except Henry. He is lunching with a few senators."

"I see."

"Savannah handed me this booklet on my way out. I fully reviewed it."

"Smart idea explaining the charts this way. So, what else do I need to know?"

"Collaboration," Deana said hopefully. "So, let's go over the itinerary for Saturday."

The waitress took food orders, returning with a plate of appetizers.

"Once everyone is seated, Millie will cover all the committees for the holidays—church plays, the birth of Christ, all of that. Once that's addressed, we will introduce our candidate.

The children will speak, then Deana. Then the question-and-answer portion. Afterwards, handshakes, and then Deana will return to the capital for vetting. Once that process happens, Henry and I will give our speech about filling the seat temporarily until next year's election."

Rosie scratched her head. "What happened to the old-fashioned campaign trail?"

"That will still happen if they don't put her in temporarily. So, this weekend will be a deciding factor."

"Who, Deana?" Rosie asked.

"Yes. So, —best behavior." Lola looked at Rosie. "Can you keep those guerrillas under control?"

Rosie's face turned a shade of crimson that looked like blood. Letting out a slow breath, she began:

"I am the matriarch of our family, as my mother was before me. We believe in death before dishonor, along with the rules in our manifesto. It is how we choose to live."

"So, this is a real and chosen lifestyle?"

"Yes, it is. I admit I read the reports filed about the events that made the mountain come down. Is that why you didn't win a political seat?"

"It was a complicated time."

"Could Rosie really have done that?" Lola asked.

Deana sighed. "She sabotaged my campaign."

Lenny cleared her throat. "Yes, I did. She is family, and as a member of the family, we decide what's best."

"Do you decide for Curtis also,?" Lola asked.

Rusty and Leroy smiled. "Want to know how we introduced ourselves?"

Shaking her head, Deana explained, "I sent paperwork with Curtis to deliver. They snuck up behind him, pulled a gun, and explained that they hunt humans the way others hunt animals."

Curtis popped in with, "At least in-country you knew who the enemy was."

"Last probationary question," Lola said. "Curtis, do you trust them?"

Letting out a breath, Curtis replied, "I was a SEAL. I was deep in-country. If I had to go to war, I'd want them next to me."

"OK. I'll see you Saturday." Lola left. She knew there would be issues with this family, they weren't the type to take orders.

Rosie looked at Deana. "She has alternative plans."

"I wouldn't be surprised," Deana said. "We'll discuss this at home. Come on, guys—we have our workouts and firearms practice."

"Lenny, you like this security detail a little too much."

Lenny admitted she did. "Lola is quite inquisitive, isn't she?"

"Yes," Deana smirked.

Lenny headed back to the office. Deana thought about both Lola's and Henry's stake in the campaign.

It sounded like a handshake made in a backroom. The board of directors also, had a stake. Too many alternative plans.

Savannah greeted Deana with several phone messages. "Looks like your clients have their own views about what you should stand for and what you can do for them."

"Well, no one asked what they wanted before. They know I'll listen."

"Who are these men in the messages?" Savannah asked.

"I think they're senators for our district. Looking for blood in the water already. I'll play nice."

"So, how did lunch go?"

"It was like a verbal chess match. She met Rusty, Leroy, and Lenny."

"Oh, that must have been interesting."

"And Rosie was there too."

Savannah chuckled. "Did Lenny do it?"

"Let me guess," Deana said. "She tried to beat scores on the gun course."

"Only a point behind you. But the boys blew the doors off your scores."

Smiling, Deana said, “Those boys have had a handgun in their hands since they could speak full sentences.”

“Sounds like the kids around here. Hunting is a big thing. The boys have a contest every year for the size, weight, and points of their buck.”

The health agencies were submitting things clients could use. The County Health Department went through its allotted budget within the first six months. Those budgets needed to be changed to reflect actual expenses.

“So, I guess I need to show this as a graph depicting what the counties need—or lack.”

Savannah brought in a fax showing which counties needed more funding. After reading the budgets carefully, Deana discovered four ways to save money and redirect it.

The more she read, the more she understood the shuffle game.

Heading home, Deana knew she'd have to change her game plan and adjust all her graphs to reflect the lack of funding for those who needed it.

Pulling into the driveway, the number of cars showed many people were there. Deana greeted her daughters and asked what they studied in school.

"Mama, where should we put Aunt Rosie's chair?"

Curtis said, "How about my place? No one ever comes over there. It's safe."

"OK, Curtis. Make sure nothing happens to it. We paid for it ourselves."

Smiling, Deana said, "I know how much you love your Aunt Rosie."

"What should we get Mama?"

"How about a picture of you two in your uniforms?"

"Yeah, I guess. But Curtis—that's not pretty."

"I think you girls look fine in your cadet uniforms. And its only Halloween—we have time to find the perfect thing."

"Are you sure, Curtis?"

"Yes, I'm sure."

Going over the new data, Deana sadly realized the poor had been underfunded for years. Population was far higher than available jobs.

Rosie sat down with tea and three fingers of scotch. "So, what is that logical brain of yours telling you?"

"They are purposely underfunding the poor population So, they move, relinquish their property, and the town can sell it."

"Now that you know they're dirty, watch your ass. There's more than Lola looking into your history. You have two days before Millie's luncheon. You can back out."

"No. I don't get intimidated by money or political office. If they think I'm backing down—let's play."

"You're aware this could mean Henry too?"

"I'm aware. Henry's intentions may be less than honorable."

Rosie Soothed, "I know how you feel, but keep your eyes on the prize. And don't fail us, AJ."

"Thanks. No pressure there, Rose."

"Not at all. Stop bitching, Deana. This is the road we're all on."

"Who would ever think there were So, many crooks out there?"

Working on her speech, Deana fell asleep at the kitchen table. Curtis looked at Rosie.

"Put her to bed and catch yourself Some sleep."

Rosie called Henry. "Our girl got her hands on old budgets."

Laughing, Henry said, "I knew she'd find them."

"Do not screw with our girl, Henry."

"I'm on Deana's side, believe it or not."

"We shall see."

Hanging up, Rosie knew this wouldn't be an easy choice.

Going to bed, she tossed and turned, dreaming of the old lady shaking her finger.

You must avenge our family members' lives.

Waking drenched in sweat, she whispered, "We need to avenge their deaths."

Rosie wrote down a few notes and tried to sleep.

Kaylin and Bobbie Sue were in the kitchen when Curtis quietly snuck in.

"What are you girls doing?"

"Trying to make coffee."

Pouring cereal with milk, Curtis left the girls busy while he made coffee.

"Mama and Aunt Rosie are still asleep."

"Sounds like a long night."

Kaylin carefully carried Aunt Rosie's coffee to wake her. A set of brown eyes looked up with a questioning expression.

"We made coffee," Kaylin said.

Rosie smiled. “OK. Please tell me there was an adult with you.”

Curtis peeked around the corner. “I found them trying to make breakfast, So, I did the coffee.”

Letting out a large sigh, Rosie said, “Thank you, Curtis.”

Savannah called, explaining Deana had many messages.

Curtis said, “She’s asleep. She fell asleep at the kitchen table.”

“Well, get her going Millie asked for a sit-down.”

“Got it.”

Curtis gently shook Deana. “You need to wake up. Millie called Savannah for a sit-down.”

“Oh shit—I overslept. I found your children trying to make coffee and breakfast.

"Oh, I am So, screwed. Here's coffee. Get dressed." Rosie looked at Deana.

"Mike came to me last night about avenging the deaths in the family," Deana muttered.

"Jesus, Rosie, I have to sit down with the family, and I need to speak with—"

Deana stopped mid-sentence, already dressed and carrying a bag full of budgets and new demands. She was exhausted before the day even began. Greeting Savannah with an armful of papers, she said, "We need to have a meeting on redoing the graphs with the new data I found."

"Yes, ma'am."

"So, what did Millie want?"

"Not sure, but I'd guess topics of conversation that are not allowed."

“Ah. Control tactics. Does Henry know she asked for a meeting?”

Suzanne smiled. “I don’t believe So,”

“Well, here’s my mock-up of the new graph, with the points in the budget data nice and big So, no one can miss them. I’ll be needing these for the luncheon. But your party—please.”

“Oh—Millie is on her way up. Make sure Henry knows she’s here.”

“She’s here. Give her a ‘C’ and I’ll join her shortly.”

After a few deep breaths, Deana walked in and offered Millie a handshake.

“So, Millie, what can I do for you? You called this meeting.”

“Let’s start with the quality of my clients. Handmade items are quite nice and worth the money.”

“Thank you. I’m sure the ladies will appreciate your views.”

“Let me tell you the whole story. One of our ladies finally made enough to purchase a toolbox for her husband and her children. She is very proud of this fact. Many of my clients are doing better.”

“So, why are you really here, Millie?”

“Well… even though you’ve done So, much for the townspeople, I would appreciate it if you did not fill the ladies up with that women’s lib stuff. We like having our men in charge. Plus, the no-mixing rule. You need to understand your place as a woman.”

Standing, Deana was winding up just like Count Submission.

Before she could open her mouth, Henry conveniently arrived.

“Well, Henry, your wife has been very forthcoming about being cared for in a patriotically talented—Henry?" Deana stammered as Millie was escorted out of the building.

Apologies came after his wife left.

"Wow, this is like robots took over last night," Deana muttered. "Do they get ordered through a speaker?"

"Oh, right now, Deana, they're old-fashioned. Not necessarily robots, but they want the 50s icons. That's what they expect life to be. TV has warped them with the massive sink."

"You were raised with a warrior as an adopted mom, a family that would rather fight than play the game."

"So, Millie wanted me to know what's expected?"

Henry nodded. "But maybe not attacking their lifestyle will get you further."

“I have graphs and data to show how the budgets are constructed for the counties. My children will talk about their experiences learning cadet skills. I’ll discuss my hopes for our town and building a stronger Montana, followed by a question-and-answer section.”

“Sounds perfectly fine.”

Rosie helped with the menu and kept a quiet place in the back So, she had a view of the whole room.

“All right, go home and practice your speech. I’ll see you Saturday. Be available by phone.”

Before leaving, Deana checked in on cases pending trial or mediation.

“Looks pretty clear-cut.”

“Let’s hope So,” Curtis replied. “So, how did it go with Millie?”

"She wanted to let me know where my place was. She believes in a patriarchal Society with men in charge."

"Oh. Please don't refer to women's rights as 'women's lib.'"

"Wow, boss, I haven't heard that in ten years."

"Millie's ideal family is basically from the 50s."

"Oh boy, boss. No wonder you rubbed her the wrong way."

Heading home, Deana saw a large campaign sign on her front lawn.

"And So, it begins." Rosie had Caitlin and Bobbie Sue writing lines: *I will never make coffee without a grownup* 100 times.

"Okay, JB's friends are willing to barter. Militia is on perimeter duty. Our Indigenous friends are teaching how to move silently through the woods and some old-fashioned but very useful skills. Bow season starts soon. Give our boys Some practice at moving targets."

"I got my hands on Some old maps and deeds to abandoned properties," JB said. "Time for a scouting mission. See how many are for sale as foreclosures."

"So, we're buying more properties?"

"We may need to. As we accept more people into our group, we'll need more room."

"Johnny, how are your wives coming with the cold-weather gear?"

"We have boxes ready to pass out. I'll order new cases of yarn for them."

"Are you ready for Saturday?"

"Yes, Deana was ready."

Rosie pulled out the cadet uniforms with badges and ribbons for their accomplishments.

"And here is yours. I purchased this too. Oh—Suzanne sent these for your daughters."

Looking them over, Deana nodded. "They're fine. I'm hoping seeing the facts will jog their consciousness."

"Bed early tonight So, tomorrow will be a good day," Deana said as she tucked her daughters in.

"Are you mad at Aunt Rosie?"

"Why would I be?"

"Because she punished you."

"We don't know why she was mad."

"Because a coffee maker is still an appliance. It gets hot, and if you spill it on yourself, you could scald your skin."

"Why didn't she explain it to us?"

"Because she expected you to know better."

"Sounds like Some miscommunication to me," Rosie said from the doorway. "I need you to listen when I speak. It's because I don't want you to be hurt. Now bed. You've got to make your momma proud tomorrow."

"Goodnight, girls."

"Now for you, Deana Jay. Let's get you settled."

"Sounds like Mike gave you a scare in your dream."

"Yes. She was pissed. We need to avenge the family deaths. But we need to know who gave the order—not the yes-men."

"That is the whole reason."

"Pouring fruit punch for a junior Congress aide... not my idea, but I'll do what it takes."

"So, you're in business with the bikers?"

"We have a good rapport with them. Careful, Rosie."

"Rosie old? You do your job and I'll do mine."

Putting the poster boards up, Deana headed to bed. As her head hit the pillow, she was out. Crazy dreams danced in her head—Henry was the one who made the order on their beloved mountain.

Sitting up, shaking, covered in sweat, she whispered, "It would kill me to find out Henry was involved."

Sleep didn't come back easily.

Rosie knocked Softly. "Moe Hunt came to visit you too?"

"No. This was Henry. He made the order to send us to hell."

"But he's never been in public office, has he?" Rosie asked.

"I don't think So, but that was a very pointed dream."

"Yes, it was. Now get Some coffee. We have a luncheon to crash."

"Coffee—me please. Irish or regular?"

"Regular."

"Girls, get in the shower."

"Yes, Mom."

After coffee, Rosie sent Deana to the shower, threatening to throw her in if she didn't move.

"I'll braid the girls' hair and fix their uniform hats."

Deana practiced her speech while hot water dripped across her face.

Looking into the mirror, she wiped off the steam, preparing herself for what could be the beginning of her political career—or the end of her legal one.

Pulling on her dress uniform with all the brass and ribbons, her hair braided, fingertips brushing her service weapon and longing to look at the sword that came with her service to her country, she grabbed her poster boards.

Lenny, Rusty, and Leroy stood there.

"Reporting for duty, ma'am."

"Wow, you cleaned up pretty good," Deana smiled. "You look sharp in full dress uniform—but you can't touch this, Lenny."

From behind Rusty and Leroy was Curtis in full military garb with all the bells and whistles. Standing in front of the stove, he smiled with pure pride as he looked at his family.

As people arrived, a few side glances came from the townswomen joining the luncheon.

Lola called the room to attention. Millie addressed the crowd, going down the list of holiday events.

Camilla introduced Deana's daughters, Caitlin and Bobbie Sue, who gave a detailed speech explaining how they learned teamwork to complete tasks. They explained the point system: after earning ten badges, you become a section leader with responsibilities to others.

They stepped forward to give out badges for medical, targets, and proper rifle usage. The ladies gave a standing ovation.

Stepping to the podium, Lola introduced Deana as the candidate for the junior senator's aide.

"Most of you know her through her Triple Crown win over Jake, who tormented this town for many years."

Deana took her place, introduced herself, discussed her military experience, and put up poster boards showing what the budgets get and where the money should be spent. She showed four places where funds could be moved to help counties, proving the towns weren't getting what they were entitled to.

Next was Curtis, explaining his teaching of the cadets and his experiences.

Then came the question-and-answer segment. The ladies seemed very uninformed about how town budgets were dispersed.

They came up to collect their booklets to share with their husbands.

Lola turned and noticed men in suits trying to hustle Deana out of the luncheon. Curtis and security demanded to know where she was going.

Lola said she was being taken to see the governor and his staff.

Curtis exploded. “No way she goes alone. It’s near the boys. How about the chick?” He smiled. “I’ll go.”

Looking at the options, they agreed to let Curtis accompany her.

After three hours of riding, Deana was led up to the county court office. After being frisked again, she was offered beverages.

“So, why am I here?”

“This is unusual,” Deana muttered. “Getting processed like this.”

“The governor wants to see where you stand on things,” the aide replied.

Deana explained how shifting the budgets would allow more needs to be covered. Henry and the board soon joined the group.

"So, Henry, what's this all about?" she asked.

With rapid-fire questions coming from every direction, Deana grew frustrated. Curtis finally broke in.

"Has she proven herself worthy? You need to get your—get your stuff together or get off the pot. If you have more questions, our next campaign staff meeting will be at the VFW for war veterans. Now take us home. Let us know what your decision is."

Henry noticed how protective Curtis had become. *Maybe there's more to this relationship than we know*, he thought.

As the car pulled up, the governor's aide walked them to the limo. Curtis opened Deana's door, noticing the aide whispering to another staffer.

"Petty business. We'll talk soon," the aide said.

As the long drive began, Deana signaled to close the window.

"So, the driver isn't listening. Yes, I am furious. How dare they drag me out of here? Yes, it's the capital of our state, but acting like it was okay to kidnap me? Oh, just wait until I see Henry at work."

Curtis waited patiently for her rant to end.

"Now that you've given your opinion," he said gently, "may I speak as Curtis?"

"Since when do you ask permission?"

"Tonight, you seemed like you needed to vent."

"So, what do you think, Curtis?"

"The rapid-fire questions tell me they were testing you. You handled them well, but your budget ideas might cause issues."

"No. I can prove they aren't taking care of their constituents. Too many are going hungry. No winter jobs. I told them the truth—illustrated with graphs and data."

"So, this vetting process is to see where you stand and whether you're on their side."

"Henry and the board had their fingers in a few of the new committee votes."

"Well, a temporary seat gets you in the door. Your prowess as a crusader will keep you in the seat."

Eventually, both Curtis and Deana fell asleep. The driver pulled into the driveway as the sun was rising.

Opening the door, Deana was greeted by several pairs of eyes—and guns at the ready.

“Are the kids up?”

“Yes. They’ll be happy to see you.”

Once the kids were sent outside to work on their float for the school parade, Curtis played the recording of the questioning—the vetting process. Deana listened to Curtis’s speech at the end.

“Nicely done, Curtis. Now we know what they expect from me. They’re trying to figure out if I’m controllable.”

Laughing, Lenny cackled. “They’ve got no idea what they’re getting into.”

“I don’t want to go into the office today,” Deana sighed.

"Go get Some rest. The office will still run without you."

She was asleep before her head hit the pillow. Curtis also, went home and went straight to bed.

Meanwhile, Rosie had brokered a deal with JB and the guys from his club. The Indigenous members were making bullets and teaching lesSons on smoking meat and skinning animals for fur. The militia was teaching preparedness and survival skills.

Lenny had the mines filled with stashes of MREs, blankets, and small arms. Gilbert gave triage lessons. All according to plan.

Next: look for abandoned properties for more camps. The wives had made and secured plenty of outdoor wear. Camouflage trucks were purchased because they needed repairs—making them more transferable for expanding troops.

As plans neared completion, Rosie knew the time was coming for planned chaos—attacks that caused distraction, confusion, and misdirection. The more troops, the more plans they could execute.

Letting out a sigh of relief—brief as it was—Rosie was interrupted by the ringing phone.

"What?" she snapped.

Henry said, "Grumpy, are we? You had our girl kidnapped and raked over the coals. So, yes, this kind of behavior pisses us off. Her children were scared."

Letting out a slow breath, Henry explained, "It was a test. To see how she handles stressful situations."

“So, a little old-boy-network test? Where is our little crusader?”

“She’s asleep, and I will not disturb her,” Rosie said firmly.

“Well, then you can tell her she passed the first vetting. We’ll be discussing putting her in the temporary seat.”

“Come up with a better way next time, or you’ll discover why I am the matriarch of this family—and why my own brothers give me respect and a wide berth.”

“Why are you So, angry, Rosie?”

“Because you’ve always lacked respect for your elders. This wasn’t done to offend you. It was just a test of her skills. Orally? No guns? Guns would have at least made it a fair fight.”

“Have no fear, Rosie. She held her own. So, did Curtis. I’ll let you know before the next test. I'm sure those guys will love her. I promise—no more kidnapping scenarios."

"Smart, Henry." Rosie smiled. "Maybe the boys should test you."

"You wouldn't."

"Who, me? I'm just an old lady."

"Now, now," Henry replied.

"Just So, we understand each other," Rosie said. "And thank your lucky stars the boys and Lenny weren't on security, or you'd have needed paramedics."

"Is that a threat?"

"No. It's a fact. I have a meeting to get to." *Click*.

Lenny came in for more glue and tacks for the float.

"What's wrong?" he asked.

"Henry thinks their test was amusing. Maybe he should get Some of his own medicine."

Curtis stood behind Lenny. "I think he should get the same treatment I got my first time with your brothers."

Rusty grinned. "I vote we have a little fun with that prick."

"Henry?" Leroy added. "Yes."

"All right," Curtis said. "But do not put Deana in a bad position with him. A gentle reminder of his place fine. But nothing that jeopardizes her."

"Yes," Lenny agreed. "What is his decision exactly?"

Planning Henry's "lesson" made Lenny smile.

"So, has anyone heard from Lola?"

"No. Why?" Rusty asked.

"I want to see if she knew about Henry's little test."

Deana woke to a full house. Rubbing her eyes, she asked, "What's wrong?"

"Henry claims last night was a trumped-up test."

"I could tell. Rapid questions, budget grilling. The governor's aide said we'd be talking soon."

Caitlin and Bobbie Sue burst in. "Mama! Our float is done! Come outside!"

Deana let them pull her to the door. Leroy covered her eyes until she reached the float. When she opened them, she saw all the important history displayed beautifully.

"Uncle Leroy and Uncle Rusty are taking it to school for the parade," the girls said proudly.

"You did a wonderful job. Followed all the rules. Aunt Lenny helped us a lot."

Covered in glue and glitter, Lenny took a modest bow. Rosie praised the float as well.

"Who else is part of yours?" Deana asked.

"It's for the cadets. Preparedness. Our rifles aren't real—we used our practice ones."

"Smart," Curtis said.

Rusty snickered. "So... steal Henry off Main Street or out of his own bed?"

Johnny laughed coldly. "Out of his own bed. That'll mess with his head. He'll never feel safe at home."

"Exactly," Leroy said.

Deana cackled. "I know nothing, Henry." An evil smile crept across her lips.

While the ladies of the church prepared for food and fellowship, the boys snuck into Henry's home. Head-to-toe in black, faces covered, they carried Henry down the stairs and out the garage. They threw him into the back of a truck covered in animal feces.

In a desolate part of the woods, they dragged him to a clearing and pulled off the mask.

Henry screamed, "What the hell are you doing? Do you know who I am? I can end your existence!"

Smacking Henry around was just good old-boy fun.

"Remember—we go hunting where you go fishing. You take your children fishing. So, be careful."

"Oh, you messed with the wrong people," Henry spat. "I never forget."

They stripped him and left him to find his way home. Rusty recorded Henry's threats.

Henry stayed off the main roads, his naked body turning a grayish blue.

At home, Deana's family enjoyed venison stew with fresh biscuits.

Sneaking back into his house, Henry knocked over the laundry soap. Millie, thinking it was a robber, grabbed a rifle and crept downstairs. Two steps into the kitchen, she flicked on the light.

"No! Don't shoot! It's me—Henry!"

"Where were you?" Millie cried.

"Lessons to be learned," Henry muttered.

"The phone has been ringing constantly. It Sounds like they've decided."

"I'll get with them tomorrow."

"Here, let me fix you a plate."

Henry ate, but his mind raced. Sleep would not come easily. He knew the lesson had been delivered for a purpose. He remembered how upset

Curtis had been about the kidnapping scenario. The questions were designed to see what needed to be done.

Even though Deana's answers were professional, there were alternative plans. Henry knew Deana would not be controlled by either party.

It was 2:00 a.m., and still no sleep. Creeping downstairs, Henry went into his study So, he wouldn't disturb the kids.

Looking at the files on his desk, he pushed them away. His views on the family had been skewed—*they really are a force to be reckoned with*.

The light on his private line lit up bright red. Henry answered.

"Hello?"

"This is your governor speaking. We've pretty well made up our minds, but we'd like to do another kind of vetting. After what happened to you, handle it yourself. I assume there were Some reprisals from her people?"

"You think those assholes stole me out of bed, took me into the woods, and gave me a warning— 'We go hunting where you go fishing'? Then they stole my clothes and I had to find my way home in the dark."

"Sounds like you had a bad evening. So, this vetting process. We'd like to visit her clients and see how they feel about Deana in public office."

"Can they read?" Henry asked.

"Yes, I believe most can. We'd like to send out Julie and Savannah."

"Why them?"

"No harm. They'd be better at disarming any doubts. I've spoken with them about the assignment. There's a list of questions—basically: Has she done well with them? Has she been honest?

Does she address concerns about employment and health care? Do they get treated fairly? Did she help them get fair wages for their work?"

"Okay," Henry said. "The questions Sound simple enough. Once we go through the data, we'll see where we end up. If we need anything else, I'll call."

"Maybe you need a day. You look bad. Normally torture does that to a man. Sleep, Henry. We've given the ladies their assignments." *Click.*

Henry flopped onto his couch, eyes fluttering shut.

He woke to find his children and the dogs staring at him.

"Are you sick, Daddy?"

"Yes, I'm feeling under the weather."

"We can stay home and take care of you!"

Smiling, he said, “Thank you for the offer, but school is important. Go get dressed.”

Millie ushered the kids away. “Honey, just go to bed.”

Henry’s thoughts drifted as he fell asleep, dreams of the town being taken over by *that* family.

Around noon, Millie knocked with a lunch tray. “You need to eat.”

Meanwhile, Deana received a visit before leaving for work. Suzanne and Julie stopped in to advise her of their assignment.

Thinking for a moment, Deana nodded. “Do what they ask. Do they have Claude on the list? He was my first defense—over a pig.”

“No, but he’ll have many good things to say.”

"What happened?" Savannah asked.

"It's a long story."

"Nothing from Henry?" Julie asked.

"He's home. Not feeling well," Deana said dryly.

After the girls left, Deana calmly called the boys for coffee. Curtis knew she had put two and two together. Rusty walked in first, Leroy behind him.

"What's up, DS?" Rusty asked.

"Is there Something you boys want to tell me?" Deana asked.

Curtis started. "Boss... I was very upset after they pulled that stunt on you."

"I see. So, whose idea was it to give Henry a lesson?"

Rusty raised his hand. "It was ours."

"Well, since he's home sick, it must've been a whopper."

Rusty shrugged. “We stole him out of his bed, took him to the woods, scared him a bit, then stole his clothes and let him find his way home in the dark.”

“Who the hell authorized this bullshit?”

Rosie stepped forward. “It was my order. I’m not going to win Mr. Congeniality, but junior senator or not, if you threaten my boss—”

“We didn’t exactly threaten him,” Leroy muttered.

“Crack,” Deana said sharply. “Leroy, what exactly did you say?”

“We just explained that we go hunting where he goes fishing.”

“Okay, that isn’t as bad as what you did to Curtis. I hear the governor is sending support staff to speak to our clients about how good I am for them. I guess they want to see how popular I am with my own people.”

"So, does that mean you have a shot at the temp seat?" Rusty asked.

"Looks like she has a shot," Leroy added.

"Were you in on Henry's lesson?" Deana asked Lenny.

"No, D. I'd have made him piss himself."

"Somehow I believe that" Deana said. "But it'll make work difficult if Henry has to worry about abduction or losing his clothes."

Rosie smirked. "I'd have paid good money to watch him find his way home."

"Lola is here!" Lenny shouted, slamming the door.

Lola strode in. "So, it Sounds like the governor is interested in you. That's why the popularity questions. And Henry is sick?"

"Yes," Deana said. "I haven't heard from him."

“Well, Millie called me. She’s requested no more of you at her functions.”

“Did I offend any of the ladies?”

“No, not exactly. It was Something to do with Henry.”

“So, why is this an issue for our girl?” Rosie asked.

“Seems your security likes practical jokes.”

“No,” Lola growled. “That was a lesson he needed to learn.”

“What was that? How to be humiliated?” Lola snapped. “Obviously this seat isn’t important enough for you to control your animals.”

Before Deana could respond, Rosie was nose-to-nose with Lola.

“This lesson was not authorized by her. It was sanctioned by me. If you have Something to say, direct it to me.”

Lola backed up slightly. "I assume it had to do with the trip to the capital."

Curtis said, "It wasn't right to pull that on Deana. Those were loaded questions with no correct answers."

"That was done to see if she could think on her feet," Curtis added. "At least in the service, the enemy was clear. Our government lives on secrets and lies. It's no place for an honest woman."

"Well, they should have an answer by the time you talk to Henry," Lola said. "It's at the VFW. No more kid games."

"I'm sure Henry will have a discussion with you, Deana."

"Not in this case," Rusty said. "I'd be more than happy to join that discussion."

Frustration tightened Lola's expression.

Deana sat at the table as Suzanne and Julie dropped off copies of all the collected data. Going through each questionnaire, she saw that most families felt treated well listened to, helped with employment options, connected with public health nurses for immunizations, birth control, and other concerns.

She had met with shopkeepers for fair pricing on handmade crafts. Claude said she handled his case with care and understood what mattered to him.

“So, does this mean you have the popular vote?” Lenny asked.

“Yes, but they haven’t talked to the militia or the Indigenous people yet. Fingers crossed.”

“Sounds like you’re on the fast track to a junior senator seat,” Rusty said.

“Let’s not count our chickens,” Deana replied. “The VFW speech is

Saturday, the ancillary on Sunday. We stick to the schedule. I'm sure after Henry regains his composure, he'll ask to see me."

Rosie snorted. "He won't run his mouth at us."

"No—he'll take it out on me. Thanks, Rusty."

"He had it coming," Rusty said. "He knew what they did, where they were taking you, and gave no warning. That's BS."

Curtis nodded. "This man thinks he's in charge. He needed to realize he can be taken out like anyone else."

"So, the data shows I'm for the people, not the wealthy blowhards in the capital," Deana said. "I understand needing the popular vote, but the governor and the board were awfully interested in what I'd do with the budgets."

"Can she be bought?" Leroy asked rhetorically. "No. She can't."

"Most of those women at the luncheon had no clue how municipalities run," Rosie said. "They never vote on budgets. It's like old Southern plantations—coming-out parties, dowries, daughters treated like prized cows."

"It's a shame these women don't know better," Deana said. "They're allowed careers and opinions."

Rosie nodded sadly. "It is a shame. Most of them are educated."

"Sounds like a women's rights campaign needs to be cracked open," Lenny said.

Clem from the militia called—they gave Deana a glowing review.

"What about the tribes?" Deana asked.

"They had to find a translator," Leroy said, "but they gave you a great review too. Even though women aren't in charge of tribal decisions, that's a home run."

Most of the town liked her. A few of Jake's old friends didn't—but that was because they no longer had a leader.

"Sounds like Deana is faring well," Curtis said. "Considering her stance on how the people from that tractor path were treated, and her platform on equality, she got a few snubs from wealthy families—but 90% agree with our girl."

Rosie thought about Henry's lesson, then decided to call him. Pulling the long phone cord into her bedroom, she sat and dialed.

On the third ring, Millie answered sweetly.

“May I speak to Henry?”

“Who is calling?”

“Rosie. He knows me.”

“He’s not feeling well. Could you call back?”

“Just ask if he will speak with me, please.”

Millie set the phone down and went into the study.

“Henry, that awful trailer-trash woman wants to speak with you.”

“Okay, I’ll pick it up,” Henry said.

“Hello?”

“Millie hung up,” Rosie said. “She didn’t Sound like she wanted to chat with me. So, —what is it, Rosie?”

“I wanted you to understand that no matter who you are, how connected you are, or how much money you have, it won't keep you safe. If I want to get to you, I will. What happened to you? I authorized a lesson, if you will. Now that I've owned up, we're square."

"Why did Savannah and Julie get that assignment?" Henry asked.

After a long, slow breath, Henry explained, "The popular vote is important. Trust matters. So, far, she's well liked."

"What is the governor up to?"

"They're close to a decision. They needed to hear from their constituents—making sure they're backing the right horse, So, to speak."

"So, they can control her," Rosie muttered. "Let's be honest—she's proudly stuck her nose in the air while breaking every rule. Henry, you can't have both ways. You can't name her the Crusader for protecting the townspeople and then tie her hands So, she can't do her job. So, what committees are you grooming her for?"

"Since she found mistakes in our county budget—money that could've been used elsewhere—that caught the governor's attention."

Rosie snarled. "The fact that Deana found it, or the fact that she bothered to read the budget and bring it to their attention?"

"Now you know as much as I do," Henry sighed. "Now a question for you, Rosie. Did Deana check in with Savannah about her cases?"

"Yes. A few court proceedings and Some mediation, but nothing urgent."

"Good. Because they could demand to see her anytime they please. Anything else?"

"That's all," Rosie said. "You're officially up to speed."

“Good evening, Rosie.” *Click.*

Henry rubbed his head as pain filled places in his mind he dared not go.

Carrying the phone back to the kitchen, Rosie gave the lowdown from Henry.

“Clem wants a meeting tonight at the compound.”

“Okay. We’ll ask for a few from each group. Eight p.m.—that way the kids are done with chores and in for the night.”

“Who’s going to watch the kids?”

Deana smiled. “I’ll stay with them. Rusty can update me later.”

“Curtis, see if you can get the chief and his second,” Rosie said.

“I’ll go get Roland,” Leroy added.

“The militia will be there. JB and his club will send delegates. Then us.”

After dinner and baths, Lenny put on a Halloween movie while the rest headed to the compound. Johnny checked fire supplies and snacks before guests arrived. Rosie inspected the hall, making sure there was seating for everyone.

As guests began to arrive, Johnny set out drinks and snacks on the long table.

Clem called the meeting to order. "First—we were concerned about those young ladies with the questionnaires, until they showed ID from the firm where Deana works."

Deana cleared her throat. "I had no idea about it. Considering what they pulled on me, I'm not surprised. They're looking to see how popular I am with my clients. As of now, I have a 90% approval rating."

"Have our plans changed?" Clem asked.

"No," Rosie said. "Just extra dance partners."

JB explained, "My club is helping with hardware. We have Ernie in the motor pool, a clerk, and a KP sergeant to help with supplies. Our tribal friends are making ammo and teaching how to make jerky. And then there's us."

Clem nodded. "What happens once she gets the position?"

"We set things in motion," Rosie said. "She'll be a good, beautiful junior senator and go through the files. Once we know who gave that order, we start the chaos effect."

"The chaos effect?" Someone asked.

"We keep them busy in one spot while we're Somewhere else. Cut off transportation and food supplies. Then start small campaigns. They wanted to send us straight to hell—I say we reciprocate."

"So, what do we do to honor the reporter who died trying to tell the truth?" JB asked.

"I say we submit the truth to his boss. Let him print it."

Clem's oldest Son burst through the door.

"What's wrong, Son?"

"I heard them saying they're going to say yes—but the guys from town are going to try to steer you off."

Curtis looked at Leroy. "Perimeter search. And a few light bulbs to light their way."

They had a place for storage of supplies and a special place for themselves.

Once everyone was present, Quinn asked, "Looks like you buried Something?"

Rusty laughed. "You might say that."

Moving the dirt away, Rusty unlatched a large door leading to a small stairwell. He hit a button, lighting what looked like an old pit. Climbing down, Clem discovered they had buried two school buses for storage and hiding.

After checking it out, Clem was impressed.

"My old lady Lenny designed this," Rusty said proudly. "Everything is about us."

JB's president admired the setup. "She'd do well in a club. Smart, tough, and sexy."

Rusty smiled. "And she's mine."

"No problem, bro. Let's go fix up a surprise for our local boys."

Clem asked, "Does Deana need extra guards?"

Giggling loudly, Rosie pulled down Deana's target sheets.

"Wow. Holy shit. She doesn't need guards. She's a better shot than most men in this town."

"Just checking, boss."

"So, when do you think we'll get a decision?" Clem asked.

"During this week," Rosie said.

As Deana headed home, she took the long way—cruising back roads, checking for company. Pulling into the driveway, the darkness felt almost creepy.

Around 2 a.m., while everyone slept, the boys were up to no good.

Rosie woke up sweating, tingling with instinct. Grabbing her favorite rifle, she sat quietly in front of her window.

A door creaked.

Turning toward her bedroom, Rosie put her finger on the trigger.

"Deana?"

"Jesus, Rosie—it's me."

Just then, the lawn lit up like an amusement park. Grabbing a man from behind, Curtis cuffed him and taped his mouth. Leroy and Rusty set off a few small bombs to scare the rest. As the intruders turned to run, they found themselves nose-to-nose with Deana.

"Hey boys. Where you going?"

Once all three were rounded up, the sheriff was called—again. Deana made the local newspaper for exercising her constitutional rights.

"Come on, boys. There's a nice warm cell waiting for you."

At 8 a.m., the phone started ringing—support staff, Henry, the board. Then a call from Millie.

"Yes, this is Millie—Henry's wife. I just wanted to check in and see if everyone's okay."

"Yes, all is good. Thank you for your concern."

"Wow, she's sucking up," Lenny said, grinning.

"Millie called your house?" Deana asked.

"Not yet. I'm sure there's more monkey signs coming."

"Did Rusty give me credit for my work?" Lenny asked.

"Yes. And JB's club president said you'd do well in the club."

"He said that?" Lenny beamed. "She is mine," Rusty added proudly.

Filled with pride, Lenny skipped with the girls to the bus stop.

"You got a call from the VFW—canceled," Lenny said. "Something about an announcement."

Deana headed for the shower, singing—until Henry burst into the bathroom.

"What the hell, Henry? I'm in the shower!"

"Hurry up and get out here!"

Throwing on overalls and a flannel shirt, Deana headed to the kitchen.

"This better be good. I don't share my nakedness with people."

Lola joined Henry. "Did you tell her yet?"

"He tried to join me in the shower," Deana said flatly.

Lola stared at Henry, confused.

Rosie walked in. "What now?"

"They had an initial vote," Henry said. "It's all plus two more votes—and you get the seat."

"When are the next votes?"

"Today."

"So, what do I do?"

"Be available."

By 6 p.m., the votes were tallied. Deana won by a landslide.

The governor wanted a live segment with all families, starting at the local news station.

The governor shook Deana's hand. "I am proud to announce that Deana J. will take the temporary position of Junior Senator. Congratulations."

And so, a war began and no one realized it was a war.

Epilogue

With Deana in public office, the family began planning for a war that could never be won by conventional means.
Return to the family as the war plans become clearer—and Soulless.

www.ingramcontent.com/pod-product-compliance
Lightning Source LLC
LaVergne TN
LVHW091119080826
845145LV00008B/1978

* 9 7 8 1 9 5 2 4 9 7 1 0 0 *